The lioness jumped and looked over her shoulder. She snarled loudly then spun round and threw her body against the wire, making it rattle violently.

The cubs woke up at once.

'Stay where you are!' Jake hissed desperately. Beside him, Rick slipped the rifle off his shoulder.

When the lioness spotted the cubs, she threw herself at the fence with new strength, grabbing at the wire with her massive paws. The cubs stared at her, blinking in surprise.

In her frenzy, the lioness shoved a front paw through a gap in the wire, wrenching her shoulder so that the wound opened and a steady stream of blood began to trickle down her flank.

Jake watched in horror. The lioness was going to kill the cubs!

Also in the Safari Summer *series*

Hunted
Tusk

Other series by Lucy Daniels,
published by Hodder Children's Books

Animal Ark

Animal Ark Pets

Little Animal Ark

Animal Ark Hauntings

Dolphin Diaries

LUCY DANIELS

SAFARI SUMER PRIDE

Illustrated by
Pete Smith

*Hodder
Children's
Books*

a division of Hodder Headline Limited

To the real Berman family, Lucy, Stuart,
Tanzen and Cory, with lots of love

Special thanks to Andrea Abbott

Thanks also to everyone at the Born Free Foundation
(www.bornfree.org.uk) for reviewing the
wildlife information in this book

Text copyright © 2003 Working Partners Limited
Created by Working Partners Limited, London W6 0QT
Illustration copyright © 2003 Pete Smith

First published in Great Britain in 2003
by Hodder Children's Books

The rights of Lucy Daniels and Pete Smith to be identified
as the Author and Illustrator respectively of the Work
have been asserted by them in accordance with the
Copyright, Designs and Patents Act 1988.

For more information about Lucy Daniels,
please visit www.animalark.co.uk

10 9 8 7 6 5 4 3 2 1

A Catalogue record for this book is available from
the British Library

ISBN 0 340 85122 8

Typeset in Palatino by Avon DataSet Ltd,
Bidford-on-Avon, Warwickshire

Printed and bound in Great Britain by Clays Ltd, St Ives plc

The paper and board used in this paperback by
Hodder Children's Books are natural recyclable products
made from wood grown in sustainable forests.
The manufacturing processes conform to the environmental
regulations of the country of origin.

Hodder Children's Books
a division of Hodder Headline Limited
338 Euston Road
London NW1 3BH

ONE

Jake Berman stopped dead behind a big boulder. Something was moving in the dense bushes just ahead. He nudged his stepdad, Rick, who nodded, signalling he'd seen it too. Hardly daring to breathe, Jake stared into the thicket, trying to spot a face, ear or even a tail that would identify what animal was hiding just metres from them. But whatever was lurking there, it was perfectly camouflaged by the thick undergrowth and mottled patterns of shade and light.

A twig cracked, the sharp *snap* amplified by the mid-morning silence of the African bush. Jake flinched. Next to him, Rick cautiously slipped his rifle off his shoulder.

Jake glanced at the gun, his heart pounding. Rick had warned him that they might well encounter dangerous animals in Musabi, the Tanzanian game reserve where the Bermans lived. Could this be a rhino or a lone buffalo perhaps, sheltering from the searing sun?

Another twig snapped. Jake braced himself for a wild animal to come bursting out of the bushes. Rick, who was the senior warden at Musabi, had told him that the worst thing to do was to turn and run. But even if Jake had wanted to, he couldn't have moved a millimetre.

There came a faint rustling from the edge of the thicket. Jake looked anxiously at Rick. Would he be able to fire a warning shot in time if the animal *did* charge them?

But instead of raising the rifle, Rick let it drop loosely by his side and grinned at Jake as a tiny golden brown antelope, barely as high as Jake's knee, tripped out daintily from behind the bushes. 'Dik-dik,' Rick whispered.

Jake smiled back, feeling his shoulders sag with relief. He'd only been living in Africa for a few weeks and he didn't think he was ready to come face to face with any of the continent's big predators just yet.

The diminutive antelope seemed unaware of Jake and Rick's presence. She nibbled at a thorny shrub, flicking her tail from side to side. Then, just behind her, there was another fleeting movement and a second dik-dik appeared, barely half her size.

'Look! A fawn,' Jake whispered to Rick.

'We're lucky to see that,' Rick observed.

The mother dik-dik took a few steps away from the shelter of the bush, her nose twitching as she sniffed the air. With her tiny fawn following her, she headed towards another thick clump of bushes. Jake could hardly see the dust-coloured dik-diks as they slipped through the tall dry grass.

Suddenly, there was a startling *whoosh* above Jake's head. He looked up in time to see a huge bird swooping down from the sky, its massive wings blotting out the sun. With a deadly accurate thrust of its mighty hooked talons, the bird grabbed the mother dik-dik and soared effortlessly back up into the air.

'What was *that*?' Jake exploded, shielding his eyes as he stared up at the bright blue sky where the bird and its prey were already just a speck. It had happened so quickly, Jake couldn't even tell what colour the bird had been.

'Martial eagle,' Rick answered grimly.

In front of them, the orphaned dik-dik was calling out in a frantic, high-pitched whistle. *Dik-dik-dik*, she bleated as she desperately looked around for her mother.

'What will happen to the fawn?' Jake asked.

Rick put a hand on Jake's shoulder, his blue eyes sympathetic. 'She won't last long, I'm afraid. Hyenas, lions, cheetahs, another eagle – there's any number of predators higher up the food chain. In fact, look over there.' He pointed to a termite mound not far away. A black-backed jackal was standing on top of it, its beady eyes fixed unblinkingly on the fawn.

Not for the first time since coming to Tanzania, thirteen-year-old Jake was struck by just how harsh life could be in the African bush. He had seen animal predators dozens of times on TV in England – lions bringing down zebra and impala, crocodiles snatching antelope, and cheetah running down gazelles. But on the small screen, the action had seemed rather remote and unreal.

The drama of the hunt was all too real to Jake since coming to live in Musabi with his mum, Hannah, and her new husband, Rick. His new home seemed a million miles away from life in Oxford where he'd stayed with his gran to finish the school year. It was hard to believe that only a few weeks ago he'd been hunched over a desk in a big, draughty hall doing exams!

Jake watched the baby dik-dik searching in the grass for her mother, unaware of the danger lurking nearby. 'Poor thing,' he murmured. 'I wish we could do something for her.'

'Yes. It can be pretty hard to stand by and do nothing,' admitted Rick. 'But we try not to interfere. Nature has to take its course, even on the reserve.'

On the termite mound, the jackal stretched, then leaped to the ground and started approaching the dik-dik in a wide arc, his fear of man apparently taking second place to his hunger.

Jake watched the jackal coming closer then abruptly looked away. 'I don't think I want to see this,' he said.

'Nor do I,' agreed Rick, hoisting his gun over his shoulder. He flashed an unexpected grin at Jake, his teeth very white in his suntanned face. 'Just for once, we'll bend the rules. I reckon we've got room for an orphaned dik-dik in our garden. Follow me.'

'You mean, we're going to rescue it?' Jake whispered in amazement, feeling a jolt of excitement and hope buzz through him.

'Yup,' said Rick. 'Come on, let's see if she'll let you pick her up.' He started to walk through the long grass towards the dik-dik.

Seeing them coming his way, the jackal spun round and slunk back to the termite mound. He slumped down in the long grass next to it, his black eyes still on the dik-dik.

The tiny fawn seemed almost paralysed by fear. She didn't move an inch when Jake bent down and closed his hands round the delicate quivering body. 'She hardly weighs a thing,' he whispered, straightening up with the baby held close to his chest.

Rick gently rubbed the antelope's long nose. 'She's very young,' he said. 'Not even two weeks old yet, I'd say. Which means we're going to have to bottle-feed her for a month or so.' He smiled at Jake. 'That'll keep you busy until term starts.'

'Shani can help,' Jake said. 'She's bound to know about feeding babies, seeing as her mum's a midwife.'

Jake and twelve-year-old Shani Rafiki had met soon after Jake arrived at Musabi. Shani's uncle, Morgan, was Rick's right-hand man, and he'd introduced the two when he heard they'd be going to the same secondary school in Dar es Salaam in the new term.

Gently cradling his precious burden, Jake followed Rick back to the Land Rover. At the boulder where they'd first caught sight of the tiny antelopes, he paused and glanced over his shoulder. The disappointed jackal had vanished. Jake scanned the sky. There wasn't a trace of the eagle and its victim either. They had disappeared into the empty blue expanse that covered the African plains.

Jake pushed open the screen door and went out on to the sun-scorched veranda. 'Bina!' he called. 'Breakfast time.'

It was three days after the eagle attack, and the orphaned dik-dik was starting to settle down in her new home.

'Bina,' Jake called again. The name meant dancer in Swahili, the local language. Shani had come up with it when she'd met the fawn for the first time.

Dik-dik-dik, *dik-dik-dik*, came the whistling reply.

He looked down to the far end of the long veranda, shielding his green eyes against the bright morning sun. He was still amazed at how strong the sun was so early in the morning. And this was winter! A huge contrast to the damp grey summer of England.

'Where are you, Bina?' Jake said. A slight movement beneath a carved wooden hippopotamus in the far corner caught his eye. Jake smiled. 'Trust you to hide so well!' He crouched down on the smooth stone floor and held out a small plastic bottle filled with milk. 'Breakfast time,' he repeated just as Bina tripped out daintily from beneath the wooden hippo. Her nose twitching, she made a beeline for the bottle in Jake's outstretched hand.

'Hey! Steady on,' Jake warned as Bina nudged hungrily at it. In her eagerness, she bumped the bottle out of Jake's hand. It landed with a bounce on the floor, knocking off the teat. Jake sighed as the milk formed a small puddle around Bina's front hooves.

Bina sniffed the milk then picked up the rubber teat in her mouth and started to munch happily.

'Hey! You can't eat that,' Jake scolded, prising the teeth-marked piece of rubber out of her mouth. He picked Bina up and tucked her under one arm. 'Let's go and get some more milk,' he said, carrying her indoors.

With Bina wriggling restlessly in his arms, Jake pushed the pantry door open. 'OK, OK,' he soothed. 'I know you're hungry.'

The dik-dik stared at him with her enormous black eyes then wriggled again. She was growing stronger already, but Rick had warned Jake that the fawn would never be able to go back into the wild. Once she was weaned, she would have to live in the large garden surrounding the Bermans' stone ranch-style house.

Jake entered the pantry, disturbing a young vervet monkey which had sneaked in through the small open window. The agile creature gave Jake a startled look then scampered back outside.

'Thief!' laughed Jake. And then he saw what the monkey had been after. Bina's powdered milk formula! The open tin was upside down on a shelf, its contents scattered around.

Jake groaned. 'Not much luck with your breakfast today, Bina.' He searched for another tin of formula but couldn't find one. 'I'd better tell Mum,' he said, carrying Bina out of the pantry.

He found his mother in her study going through a series of photographs which she'd taken at a water hole. Hannah Berman was a freelance journalist and wildlife photographer, and had moved to Tanzania after her marriage to Rick last year.

Hannah looked up from her desk, pushing her long black hair away from her face. 'Hi there, Bina,' she said, reaching out with one hand to stroke the dik-dik's long nose. 'How are you this morning?'

'Still hungry,' Jake said, then described the two mishaps with the milk. 'Is there another tin somewhere?'

'Yes, but not here. I arranged for some more to be delivered to the store,' Hannah answered. 'Let's hope it's arrived. Otherwise,' she scratched the top of

Bina's head, 'there's going to be one ravenous dik-dik in our midst.' She put the photographs in their envelope then picked up a bunch of keys. 'Luckily for you, Bina,' she added, 'we're going to the village anyway this morning to pick up Shani.'

Shani lived in Sibiti, a small village where her mother was the nurse and midwife. Apart from the clinic which Mrs Rafiki ran, the only other public buildings in the village were a small primary school and the Sibiti Trading Store which stocked everything from pots and paraffin to bananas and bolts of cloth, and, lately, powdered milk formula for orphaned dik-diks!

Jake took Bina back to the veranda, which was conveniently surrounded by a low wall. This kept her from straying into the garden and getting lost, although Jake knew that it was only a temporary safety measure. By the time she'd learned to jump over the wall, the little antelope would be reasonably territorial, so she'd be able to graze on the lawn without wandering off. She'd also be too big to squeeze through the game-proof fencing that surrounded the garden.

'Ready?' asked Hannah, coming on to the veranda. She put on her sunglasses and wide-brimmed hat then crossed the lawn to the car port where the green open-topped Land Rover was parked. On its front doors was the bright yellow Musabi logo of a lion beneath a spreading umbrella tree.

Jake, being tall, hopped easily over the wall and ran after his mum, trying hard to ignore Bina's distressed and hungry call. *Dik-dik-dik*, she whistled over and over again.

'Don't worry,' said Hannah, seeing Jake glance anxiously back at Bina. 'She won't starve between now and when we get back.'

Sibiti lay forty kilometres north of Musabi along a dusty, rutted road. The journey took almost an hour and a half, and longer when it rained, according to Rick. But even though it was a bone-shaking ride, Jake hadn't grown tired of it. Vast plains stretched on both sides as far as the eye could see, and he had often seen giraffe and wildebeest loping across the road just ahead of the Land Rover.

As a backdrop to this huge expanse of land, a mighty blue-grey mass rose up against the sky on the far north-eastern horizon, its peak covered by clouds. This was Kilimanjaro, the highest mountain in Africa. Jake was determined to make it to the summit one day.

* * *

It was only nine o'clock when they arrived in Sibiti, but already the sun was high in the sky. 'It's going to be a scorcher today,' said Hannah, turning into the narrow track leading to Shani's house.

'You mean another typical winter's day,' Jake teased. 'Hot and dry.' He was still trying to get used to the idea that here in the southern hemisphere, not far from the equator, there wasn't much change in temperature from one season to the next. Instead there was a dry season and a wet season and right now, in July which was really winter, they were in the middle of the dry period.

Ahead of them, half a dozen small boys were playing football in the middle of the road. They scattered to the sides as the Land Rover approached, waving and calling out greetings in Swahili. *'Jambo habari?'* they chorused cheerfully, asking Jake how he was.

Thanks to Shani, Jake could already speak a bit of Swahili. *'Mzuri sana,'* Jake called back. 'I'm fine, thank you.'

Hannah pulled up in front of the Rafikis' house. It was painted light blue and had a flat tin roof. A short-haired brown mongrel heard the Land Rover arriving and came running out, his tail wagging.

'Hi, Bweha,' Jake said, jumping down. He patted the dog, whose name meant jackal, then went to knock on the front door which was standing wide open. 'Shani?' he called into the dark interior. 'Are you ready?'

'Just coming,' came the reply.

Jake leaned against the wall and waited. A radio inside was playing a catchy tune. Jake soon found himself tapping his foot in time to the beat.

'Great music, isn't it?' Shani chuckled, coming out just then.

'Yeah,' Jake grinned, feeling a bit embarrassed.

'It's the Tanzanian Troopers,' Shani told him. 'They're my favourite group.' She gave Bweha a parting pat then climbed into the Land Rover. Jake hopped in beside her. '*Jambo*, Mrs Berman,' said Shani.

'Hi, Shani,' replied Hannah. 'Is your mum home?'

'No, She left for the clinic about half an hour ago,' Shani answered. 'Did you want to speak to her?'

Hannah started the engine again and began reversing in the narrow road. 'I just wanted to see if she had any spare rubber teats. Bina chewed the last one this morning,' she explained, backing slowly towards a steep bank on the other side of the road.

'How did she do that?' asked Shani.

'Very easily,' Jake told her, pulling a face.

Shani smiled. 'The greedy little thing. We should have called her *lafi*.'

'Or *njaa*,' Jake returned, hoping that he'd managed to pronounce the word meaning hungry. 'Because that's what she's going to be by the time we get back.'

'Well, we can save a bit of time if I drop you two off at the store to buy the milk while I go round to the clinic to pick up the teats,' said Hannah, changing into first gear and heading down the road again.

Sibiti Trading Store was the focal point of the village, where people gathered to chat on the shady veranda or under the huge fig tree just outside.

Hannah dropped off Jake and Shani, giving them some Tanzanian shillings to pay for Bina's feed, then went on to the clinic.

'Let's hope the milk has arrived,' Jake said as he and Shani went up the short flight of steps to the veranda.

Inside the store, they had to wait for a moment while their eyes adjusted to the gloom. Jake was fascinated by the shop. It was totally different from any supermarket he'd been to in England. Big sacks of beans and grains were stacked on the floor, while on the shelves behind the long counter there was a bewildering assortment of goods like transistor radios, batteries, combs, tinned milk, bread, exercise books and even a portable TV set. Suspended from the roof were zinc buckets, plastic bowls and a couple of tyres, while in one corner, next to a heap of suitcases, was an upright fridge containing soft drinks and locally brewed beer. A rich smell filled the air, a heady combination of paraffin, flour, soap and coffee.

Behind the counter the storekeeper, Julius Gorongo, stood with his arms folded across his round belly. '*Jambo*, my two young friends,' he smiled. '*Habari ya siku nyingi?*'

'We're fine,' Shani told him.

'We've come for the milk formula for the dik-dik,' Jake added.

Julius rested his chin in one hand and frowned. 'Milk formula? Let me think ... Ah, yes. It came yesterday with the maize. Wait just one minute,' he said and disappeared to the back through a beaded curtain.

Jake and Shani went to sift through a pile of CDs near the drinks fridge while they waited for him to return. Jake was about to pick up one by the Tanzanian Troopers when he heard an American-accented voice behind him. He turned and saw a young dark-haired woman dressed in khaki shorts and a white T-shirt talking to one of the customers waiting at the counter.

'Do you know if there's a telephone that I can use?' she asked. She held up a mobile phone and shrugged. 'There's no signal for this round here.'

The customer pointed to a public phone that was partly hidden by the pile of suitcases next to the fridge. A handwritten notice above it said, *Simu – Telephone*.

'Thanks,' said the woman. She went over to it, passing Jake and Shani on her way so that Jake was able to see a logo on the back of her T-shirt. Alderton Productions, it read.

Since he'd been in Tanzania, Jake had come across a lot of visitors – mostly tourists from America or Europe on safari with tour operators. Apart from their accents and appearance, it was easy to tell that they were visitors because most of them wore T-shirts bearing the names of tour companies, like African Adventures Unlimited and Tanzanian Treks.

'I haven't seen that name before,' Jake remarked quietly to Shani, nudging her.

Shani glanced at the visitor's T-shirt. 'Nor have I.'

The woman took out some coins then dialled a number that she looked up in a small notebook.

'Hello,' she said, dropping the coins into the slot. 'Is that Rungwa Wildlife Sanctuary?'

Jake and Shani exchanged surprised looks. They'd been to Rungwa with Rick only a few days ago to see a pair of cheetahs that a cattle rancher had tried to poison. Cheetahs were endangered animals and the sanctuary had found them just in time. Jake guessed that the American was another reporter coming to do a feature on the pair.

'This is Sophie Walker,' continued the woman.

The person at the other end of the line clearly wasn't expecting her call because Sophie had to repeat herself. 'Walker,' she repeated firmly. 'Sophie Walker. From Alderton Productions. I was in touch with someone at the sanctuary earlier this year.'

Sophie listened to the reply then said, 'Yes. Alderton Productions from California. We've finally arrived in Tanzania and would like to come and fetch the two babies you promised us.'

Jake felt puzzled. Sophie didn't seem to be a journalist after all. And who were the babies she was talking about?

Shani was similarly intrigued. She frowned at Jake and mouthed silently, 'Babies? From Rungwa?'

Julius came rattling back through the bead curtain and waved two tins in Jake's direction. 'Coming,' said Jake, putting down the CD. He took a step towards the counter but was stopped dead in his tracks by what Sophie said next.

'But of course you know which babies I'm talking about, Mr Masata,' she insisted. 'The two cubs. The lion cubs you said we could use for our movie.'

TWO

Jake listened, fascinated, as Sophie continued her telephone conversation.

'What do you mean we can't have them any more?' she asked. Her bewildered expression turned into a look of dismay. 'But I don't understand,' she protested. 'In the fax you sent us in April you promised that everything had been arranged. And now you're saying the cubs are no longer available?' She fiddled anxiously with the telephone wire. 'This puts us in a very awkward situation. Filming is due to start in a couple of days, but without the cubs that will be impossible. Are you *sure* they're too old now?' she tried one last time.

The response was clearly not the one Sophie wanted. She sighed with exasperation as she hung up.

Jake was burning with curiosity. A movie, here in Sibiti! Itching to find out more, he stepped forward, trying to think of a way to ask questions without seeming nosy.

But Shani beat him to it. She pulled a pack of chewing gum out of her pocket and offered a piece to Sophie. 'Hi,' Shani said with a grin. 'Would you like some gum? You look very worried about something.'

Surprised, Sophie looked round at Shani, then smiled as she accepted the gum. Thank you,' she said. 'And you're right. I'm in big trouble.'

'Because of the lion cubs?' Jake put in quickly. Outside, a car pulled up. Jake glanced out of the door, hoping it wasn't his mum yet. But it was only two men getting out of an old pick-up.

Sophie nodded. 'That's right. You see, I'm the animal handler for a movie company . . .' She paused and twisted round a little way to show them the logo on her T-shirt. 'And we're all set to start filming our latest production, which features a pair of cubs – only now we don't have any cubs.' She moved aside to let the two men from the pick-up up go past her to the drinks fridge.

'Why did Rungwa promise to let you have the lions if they're too old?' Jake asked.

'Well, it's all a big mix-up,' Sophie answered, running a hand through her hair. 'You see, we planned to arrive in Tanzania at the beginning of May, but there were some unexpected delays. If we'd come in May, everything would have been fine. The cubs, a pair of orphans, were only three months old then and could still be handled easily. But Mr Masata says that now they're five months, they're too big.'

'Does that mean they're dangerous?' Jake asked.

'Well, they're certainly not tame enough to use in a movie,' Sophie told him. 'When we didn't turn up to claim the cubs, the sanctuary put them on a rehabilitation programme, with minimum human contact.'

'So that they can go back into the wild when they're bigger?' asked Shani.

'I guess that's the idea,' Sophie replied. She shook her head, clearly annoyed with herself. 'We should have phoned Rungwa when we knew we'd be late. We might have been able to persuade them to keep handling the cubs until we arrived.'

'What are you going to do now?' Jake asked.

'Try to find another pair of cubs, I guess,' said Sophie. 'But the problem is, where?'

Drinking from their bottles of coke, the two men passed in front of them again, pausing for a moment to look at the CDs before going to pay at the counter.

'Can't you make the movie without the cubs?' Shani asked Sophie. 'I mean, if you go into the game parks, you'll be able to film lots of lions there.'

Sophie smiled. 'I wish it was as easy as that. But the cubs have to interact with the main characters in the movie – handling, feeding, playing, that sort of thing.' She looked at her watch. 'Well, I guess I'd better get going and see what I can arrange. One thing's certain, though. Mr Alderton isn't going to be too thrilled at the news!' She turned to go. 'Thanks for listening – and for the gum,' she added, heading for the door.

Jake and Shani watched her leave then went across to the counter and waited while the storekeeper attended to the two men.

'What a mess,' Jake commented. 'Imagine bringing a whole movie company all the way from America only to find you can't make the movie!'

Shani shrugged. 'Too bad!' she said, sounding unsympathetic as she stepped aside to let the men go past her.

Jake felt a bit taken aback. Shani could be direct at times, but she wasn't usually so abrupt. 'I'm glad you didn't tell Sophie that,' he remarked, taking the shillings out of his pocket and giving them to Julius.

'I wouldn't have done that,' Shani grinned. 'But let's just say I'm very happy for the cubs.' On the counter next to her was a heap of plastic fly swats. She picked one up and tapped Jake on the shoulder with it. 'Roll over!' she said sternly.

'What?' Jake ducked away and frowned at Shani, whose dark eyes were twinkling mischievously. 'What are you doing?' he asked.

Julius laughed. 'She's training you, my friend,' he told Jake. 'Like a lion cub.'

'One that has to learn unnatural tricks,' Shani elaborated. She put down the fly swat then, with her hands on her hips, said solemnly to Jake, 'I mean, if you were a lion, would you like that kind of life? Or would you rather live in the bush?'

Jake hadn't thought of this before, but he could see her point. 'I guess you're right,' he told her.

There was a toot outside. Jake recognized the sound of the Land Rover's horn. 'That's Mum,' he said. 'Let's go.' He smiled at Julius. 'Bye, Mr Gorongo. Thanks for the milk.'

'Kwaheri,' said the storekeeper with a wave of his hand. 'See you again soon.'

Jake and Shani hurried outside and climbed into the Land Rover.

'Well done,' said Hannah, seeing the tins of

formula. 'And we've got four spare teats, thanks to Shani's mum. That should keep Bina going for a while.'

'Unless the monkey gets into the store room again,' Jake pointed out. He fastened his seat belt then looked across the road. Sophie was sitting in a small green jeep, talking to the two men who'd left the shop ahead of Jake and Shani. One of the men wrote something on a piece of paper which he gave to Sophie. She put it in her pocket then nodded at the men and started up the motor.

'Bye, Sophie!' Shani called out, waving to her.

Sophie looked across and waved back, then drove away quickly.

'Who was that?' asked Hannah.

'An American animal handler, from a film company,' Jake told her. He explained what he and Shani had learned. 'I wonder where they'll be making the movie?'

Hannah was about to turn the keys in the ignition but she stopped and looked at Jake. 'Actually,' she said with a smile, 'I can tell you exactly where the location is.'

'Where?' Jake and Shani asked in unison.

Hannah's smile broadened as she said, 'In Musabi.'

'Musabi!' Jake echoed.

'Uh-huh. Rick and I were going to tell you once the film camp had been set up,' explained Hannah. 'The producer, Hank Alderton, has offered to take you on a tour of the set when it's ready.'

'Cool!' Jake exclaimed.

'Sounds great,' Shani agreed cautiously. 'But maybe there won't be much to see now. It sounds like the cubs were the real stars. Remember, Sophie said that without them the movie can't be made.'

Hannah started the engine and pulled away from the kerb. 'I doubt that will happen. After the expense of bringing the company all this way, I expect they'll do everything to find a replacement pair of cubs,' she said. She braked to allow a straggly herd of goats to scamper across the road in front of the Land Rover.

'But where?' Jake asked. 'It's not as if you come across tame cubs every day.'

The goats ran up the stony embankment on the other side of the road then stood at the top watching the Land Rover go past.

'Yes, and Rungwa is the only wildlife sanctuary anywhere near here,' Shani pointed out.

Hannah nodded in agreement. 'Maybe Sophie has some other contacts,' she suggested.

They left the village and headed out into the savannah. Jake gazed out at the wide open space all around them. It seemed almost endless, and a lot of it, Jake knew, was protected by game reserves. Alderton Productions could have chosen any of a dozen places to make their movie. *But they chose Musabi*, Jake thought with a thrill of excitement. He just hoped that the movie would go ahead.

THREE

'Who's that at this time of the morning?' wondered Rick, pushing back his chair and standing up to get a better look at the jeep coming up the drive.

It was two days later and the Bermans and Shani were having breakfast under a gazebo in the front garden. Bina skipped daintily around their feet, tasting the grass and sniffing hopefully at her empty bottle on the ground.

'Maybe it's someone from the film company,' Jake suggested. He stuffed the last slice of mango into his mouth then followed Rick across the lawn to the top of the drive.

The jeep pulled up in front of them. 'Morning, folks,' said the smiling driver in a broad American accent.

'Good morning,' replied Rick. 'What can we do for you?'

Before the visitor could reply, Shani came over with Bina in her arms. 'Have you come to tell us we can go to the movie set?'

The man smiled and reached out to pat the dik-dik. 'I sure have,' he said. 'Mr Alderton would be very happy for you to come and have a look around any time today. I'm on my way to town right now, but I could pick you up on my way back.'

'Or Rick could give us a lift,' Jake said, turning to his stepdad. 'You can drop us on your way to Chozi, can't you, Rick?'

Chozi was a forested area of Musabi that Rick was monitoring for snares.

'Sure.' Rick nodded, running a tanned hand through his thick blond hair. 'And I wouldn't mind having a look round the film set myself.'

'That sounds fine,' said the American and, with a cheerful wave, he started back down the drive.

'What was that all about?' asked Hannah when the others returned to the table.

Jake told her. 'I suppose if they're ready to start filming, they must have found some more cubs,' he added.

'So quickly?' remarked Shani, putting Bina on the ground.

'Maybe Rungwa had another pair of orphans after all,' suggested Hannah.

'I'd say that's pretty unlikely,' said Rick thoughtfully, pouring more coffee into an oversized mug. 'You don't come across young orphaned cubs every day. Still, if Alderton has found another pair, I'd like to check them out. I also want to make sure they're properly handled.' Born and educated in England, Rick had been a leading big cat expert at London Zoo before coming to Tanzania five years ago. He swallowed the last mouthful of coffee and put on his sunglasses. 'Right then, you two,' he said to Jake and Shani. 'Ready to go?'

'You bet,' said Shani, abandoning the slice of toast she was buttering and jumping to her feet.

Rick picked up his rifle and slung it over one shoulder. He bent down to kiss Hannah. 'You sure you don't want to come and see the camp too?'

'Another time,' said Hannah. She reached down to stroke Bina, who was nibbling a blade of grass. 'I want to finish that piece I'm doing on dik-diks for the *British Wildlife Journal*.'

Jake and Shani climbed into the front seat of the Land Rover next to Rick. They set off down the dusty drive, and turned on to the main road, jerking to a halt almost immediately when a mongoose dashed out in front of them, a thin green snake dangling from its mouth.

'No road sense!' grinned Rick, driving on again after the little animal had dived back into the bushes.

Alderton Productions had been allocated an area of the reserve that was several kilometres from the Bermans' house on the flood plain of the Ngala river that marked the boundary between Musabi and its western neighbour, the Kasaba game reserve. During the wet season, the Ngala flowed strongly, spilling out over the flood plain and cutting the two reserves off from one another. But now, in the dry season, it was just a shallow stream, easily crossed by the wildlife.

They approached the camp along a dirt road that meandered down a gentle hillside into the river valley. From the top of the hill, Jake could see about a dozen safari-green tents set up in the shade of some towering fever trees. Several jeeps and pick-ups were parked nearby, while on the far side of the site, a team of men was putting the finishing touches to a bungalow which looked like a smaller version of the Bermans' house. Its walls were made of stone and there was a shady veranda along the front.

Shani stared at it in astonishment. 'Did they build a special house just for Mr Alderton?' she asked.

Rick laughed. 'No. He'll be staying in one of the tents, like everyone else. That house is just a wooden set, painted to look like stone.'

Rick parked the Land Rover alongside the other vehicles, then the three of them made their way to the tented area. They passed a khaki-uniformed man who was leaning against a tree with a rifle slung over his shoulder. As soon as he saw them, the man stood to attention and saluted, smiling broadly.

Rick saluted in return. '*Jambo habari?* Any dangerous animals in camp so far?'

'*Njema*,' said the man, shaking his head. He was one of four wildlife guards – *askaris* – that Rick had posted to patrol the site to ensure the safety of the film crew and actors. Like all the surrounding reserves, Musabi was home to the 'big five' – lions, elephants, buffalo, rhino and leopards. 'I think all the noise and movement has made them cross the river to Kasaba,' said the askari.

'Well, keep your eyes open,' grinned Rick. 'You never know when a leopard or a hyena might want to come and share Mr Alderton's barbecue!'

'Is that him over there?' Jake asked, noticing a broad-shouldered, dark-haired man sitting with his back to them in a canvas chair. Printed in large letters on the back of the chair was the word PRODUCER.

'Yup, that's him,' confirmed Rick. 'Let's go and tell him we're here.'

The producer turned round when he heard them approaching. 'Well, hello there,' Mr Alderton beamed, standing up and stretching out his hand to Rick. 'Great to see you again.' He shook Rick's hand vigorously, his chunky gold watch rattling loudly. 'And you must be Jake and Shani,' he said, smiling at them.

'That's right,' Jake replied. 'Thanks for offering to show us around.'

'No problem,' said Mr Alderton. 'Come this way.' He led them across to the temporary house. 'We're filming all the outdoor scenes here in Musabi,' he told them. 'But we'll be shooting the indoor takes in our studios in Hollywood.'

'Hey!' exclaimed Shani, going through the bungalow's front door. 'There's nothing in here. And there's no roof. It's like a cyclone blew everything away. It's just a *fake* house.'

Laughing, Mr Alderton explained. 'It's because we need only the façade for the outdoor footage. We've built lots of sets back home to look like the interior of the house.'

'Does that mean that most of what we see on a screen isn't real?' Jake asked.

'You got it,' grinned Mr Alderton. 'It's nothing but plaster of Paris, cardboard, and clever lighting to trick you into thinking you're watching the real McCoy.'

'The real *what*?' Shani frowned.

'The real McCoy,' Jake repeated. 'It's a slang way of saying the real thing.'

'Real McCoy,' Shani chuckled. 'I like that.' Then, as Rick and Mr Alderton walked on a few paces ahead, she said in the softest whisper, 'Let's hope the lion cubs they use will be fakes too!'

Jake nodded. Shani's suggestion made sense. 'That's not a bad idea. They could use robots made to look like lions. Or even animatronics.'

'Anima-whatics?' Shani frowned.

'Animatronics,' Jake repeated, recalling a TV programme he'd seen. 'They're sort of life-size models with actors inside.'

'That sounds perfect,' said Shani.

Mr Alderton took them over to a small group of people standing next to a steel object that looked like a crane on wheels with a massive camera at the top. 'This is the camera crew,' he said. He introduced them to the Director of Photography, a slight young woman called Caron Lucas, and her two assistant cameramen.

'What's this for?' asked Shani, pointing to the crane.

'It's a crab dolly,' Caron explained. She hoisted herself on to a seat halfway up the arm of the crane. 'This is where the camera operator sits. He can raise or lower the camera like this.' She pulled on a lever and the arm of the dolly rose until the camera was about a metre from the ground.

'Why is it called a *crab* dolly?' Jake asked.

'Because it can move like a crab in any direction, even sideways,' answered one of the assistant cameramen with a grin. To demonstrate, he pushed the dolly back and forth and whizzed it round in circles until Caron, who was still sitting on it, cried out,

'Enough, Sam! You're making me dizzy!'

Shani was fidgeting with the colourful bead bracelet she always wore. 'Where are the actors?' she asked, sounding puzzled. 'I thought they'd be all over the place.'

'And what about the cubs?' added Rick, glancing around. 'Did you find another pair?'

'Well, we don't have the full cast out here,' Mr Alderton explained, looking at Shani. 'Just a couple of the principal actors and few extras and—' But before he could go on, he was interrupted by a high-pitched yell.

'Daddeeee!'

The ear-piercing shriek made a pair of rock pigeons perching in a nearby tree scatter in alarm. Everyone looked across to where the voice was coming from. A little girl of about eight was racing towards them at top speed, her mop of golden ringlets bouncing. 'Look, Daddy,' she cried. 'Look what I found.' In one hand she held a black and white spine with a sharp end, like the central part of a feather.

'Hello, sweetheart,' smiled Mr Alderton, bending down and folding the little girl into a hug as she reached him. 'That's a porcupine quill,' he told her, examining the sharp spine. 'Well done, honey. Now all we need to do is find the rest of the animal,' he teased, his eyes twinkling. Straightening up again he looked at Jake and the others. 'This is my daughter, Raquel,' he said proudly. 'A star of the future.'

'Are you in the movie?' Shani asked the little girl.

'Oh, yes. I have a walk-on part,' came Raquel's rather aloof reply, before she started tugging impatiently at her father's arm. 'Daddy, I want to see Marigold and Marmaduke again. Take me to them now,' she demanded.

Jake couldn't imagine his mum letting him speak

like that. Raquel was obviously thoroughly used to getting exactly what she wanted.

Raquel jumped up and down at her father's side. 'Please, please, pleeease,' she whined. 'I want to see my Marigold and Marmaduke again. Now!'

'OK, honey,' said her father. 'We'll go there right this minute.' He turned to Rick. 'I think you'll want to meet them too.'

'Oh, right?' Rick said, looking politely interested. 'Who are they?'

'They're my new friends,' butted in Raquel. 'I'll show them to you.' She grabbed her father's arm and marched him towards a green shade cloth on the edge of the camp.

Jake wondered who could be behind the cloth. Maybe some really famous actors who wanted privacy? He was completely unprepared when he rounded the screen.

'Lions!' he exclaimed, staring in amazement at two very young cubs playing in a large enclosure. Ignoring their audience, the baby lions scuffled energetically, nipping each other with sharp teeth that already looked capable of causing a nasty bite.

Jake turned to Shani, who looked just as surprised as him. 'So they managed to find another pair after all,' he said.

Shani gazed at the tumbling pair then said softly, 'No fake ones, these.'

'No,' Jake agreed. 'They're the real McCoy.'

FOUR

The cubs rolled and tumbled together, batting each other clumsily with paws that seemed too big for their bodies.

'They're like overgrown kittens,' Jake laughed. 'Spotted ones too,' he added, noticing the mottled, almost leopard-like spots on their tawny coats.

'They're not kittens. They're baby lions. And they're mine!' Raquel said bossily. She pointed to the bigger of the cubs. 'That one's Marmaduke and the other one is Marigold.'

Jake turned to his stepdad. 'How old are they?' he asked.

'About six to eight weeks,' Rick estimated, crouching down and looking at the pair through the strong wire-mesh fence. 'They're in good shape, too.'

The cubs paused in their play and stared inquisitively at him. Then, with ears pricked, they padded over on their short, stocky legs to inspect him. Jake and Shani knelt down quietly next to Rick and watched the pair come closer.

When the cubs were just an arm's length away, they stopped and stared at their audience. Suddenly, Marmaduke pounced on his sister, bundling her against the fence.

It was the closest Jake had ever been to a lion! He felt an urge to touch the cub's thick coat through the wire. He reached out just in time to feel the soft woolly fur before Marigold sprang away and launched herself at her brother. Marmaduke fell to the ground with a thud, a cloud of dust rising up around him. Marigold landed on top of him and grabbed the loose skin around his neck in her jaws.

'She's a feisty little thing,' smiled Rick, standing up and dusting off his hands.

Just then, Raquel poked the porcupine quill through the wire and waggled it excitedly. 'Look, Marigold and Marmaduke!'

Startled by the sudden movement, the cubs stopped. They hissed loudly at Raquel, flattening their ears and opening their mouths in a silent growl.

'Careful, honey,' warned Hank, pulling Raquel away from the wire. 'Remember, they're still learning who we are.'

'But I want to play with them,' protested the child.

'Later. When they're more settled,' Hank told her.

Rick raised his eyebrows in surprise. 'They're pretty wild,' he said. 'They can't have had much exposure to humans.' He looked up at the producer. 'Where did you find them, Hank?'

'Actually, it was Sophie who found them,' Mr Alderton replied, his arm firmly around Raquel's shoulders.

Jake shot Shani a look. 'But I thought the Rungwa lions were too big?' he blurted out.

Hank didn't ask how Jake knew about the Rungwa cubs. 'Yes, the original ones were too big,' he admitted. 'But Sophie had a stroke of luck. She bumped into some people who said they'd rescued an orphaned pair and were looking for a good home for them.'

'Really?' queried Rick. 'We don't come across orphaned cubs very often. What happened to the mother?'

'Apparently she died from a serious injury,' said Hank. 'But Sophie can give you all the details. There she is now.' He beckoned to Sophie who had appeared at the far side of the enclosure with a tall, handsome man wearing dark glasses and a baseball cap.

Sophie came round to where the others were, leaving her companion watching the cubs from the other side. 'Hi, there,' she said, recognizing Jake and Shani. 'What brings you two here?'

'I live at Musabi,' Jake explained, unable to hide the note of pride in his voice. 'Rick's my dad.'

Sophie folded her arms and smiled. 'Isn't that a coincidence?' she said. She glanced at the cubs, who had flopped down side by side under a tree. 'Aren't they the most gorgeous little creatures?' she said tenderly. 'And just perfect for the movie.'

'Where did you find them?' Rick asked, his voice echoing his concern for the cubs.

'Well, that was another coincidence,' answered Sophie. She looked at Jake and Shani. 'I don't know if you remember seeing two men in the store the other morning?'

'The ones who came in to buy cokes?' Jake clarified.

'And then went to talk to you in your jeep?' added Shani.

Sophie nodded. 'That's right. Russell Lawson and Lyle Havers. It turned out that they're rangers at Kasaba. They told me they saw a buffalo kill a lioness last week.'

'A buffalo can kill a lion?' Jake butted in, amazed.

'Oh, yes,' Rick told him. 'Especially when a lioness is hunting alone.'

'I thought lions always hunted in packs,' said Shani.

'Usually, they do. But a lioness leaves her pride to give birth and only goes back with her cubs when they're about six or seven weeks old,' Rick explained. He turned to Sophie again. 'You were saying . . .?'

'Just that Havers and Lawson saw the kill then came across the cubs,' said Sophie.

'And by chance, they overheard you in the shop then sold you the cubs,' said Rick, sounding rather sceptical.

'Well, yes. That's how it was,' said Sophie. She looked at the cubs and frowned. 'It's unfortunate about their mother, but at least we can take good care of them.'

'Do you think they ever wonder where their mother is?' mused Shani.

'Who knows?' said Rick. 'Although they seem happy enough for the time being.'

'Much happier than if they'd been left alone in the bush,' Jake pointed out. 'The hyenas would have had them by now.'

'That's true,' Rick said, thoughtfully. 'But I'm surprised the warden at Kasaba allowed Havers and

Lawson to sell the cubs. The usual thing would be to take them to Rungwa. Still, I suppose the Kasaba team was glad to find someone who'd look after the cubs well.' He glanced at his watch. 'I'd better be on my way to Chozi. See you two in a couple of hours,' he said to Jake and Shani. 'I hope all goes well with the filming,' he added, nodding to Hank. Then he walked across to the Land Rover, waving to the askari as he passed.

After Rick had gone, Jake turned to Sophie. 'What's going to happen to the cubs when you've finished with them?'

'I've spoken to Rungwa about that,' replied Sophie. 'They'll take them when we go back to the States.'

Hearing Sophie's words, Raquel burst out angrily, 'They're not going to Rungwa. They're coming home with me.'

The outburst silenced everyone for a moment. Shani spoke up first. 'The lions belong in Africa, Raquel. Not in California.'

'I don't care. Marigold and Marmaduke are *mine*,' insisted Raquel, stamping her foot in the dust. 'And Daddy promised me I could take them home.' She tugged on Hank's arm. 'Didn't you, Daddy?'

Hank looked a little embarrassed. Raquel continued to tug at his arm until he threw up his hands and grinned sheepishly. 'OK. OK. Don't fret, Raquel. I did promise we'd take the cubs home and we will. They'll have a great life with us – even better than they'd have at Rungwa.' Warming to the idea, he spelled out the plans he had for Marigold and Marmaduke. 'We'll build them a brand new enclosure on the ranch, and you'll be able to see them every day, honey.'

'See?' Raquel said smugly, turning to Shani. 'They're going to be very happy with us.'

Shani gave a brief smile, and went to stand in the shade of a nearby umbrella tree to watch the cubs. Marigold lifted her head and looked around, then rolled on to her side and started licking her brother's head.

Jake wandered over to join Shani. 'I guess if the cubs have got to be in captivity, it makes no difference whether they end up in a sanctuary in Tanzania or on a ranch in California,' he pointed out. 'Maybe they'll even be better off with the Aldertons, seeing as they're so wealthy.'

'Maybe,' Shani shrugged, following the producer with her eyes as he walked away towards the film set.

The cubs stood up and stretched then padded over to drink from a big tin tub. They drank messily, seeming to spit out more water than they swallowed. When she'd finished, Marigold climbed into the tub and began splashing about with her front paws, spilling water on to the ground. Marmaduke sat back and watched her quizzically for a moment. He sniffed at the muddy puddle surrounding the tub then flopped down in it and rolled around until his golden coat was a soggy dark brown mess.

Shani laughed. 'He doesn't look much like a film star now!'

A few metres away, Sophie was laughing too. 'He couldn't have chosen a worse time to do that,' she called over to Jake and Shani. 'It looks like Pete has come to fetch them for their first scene!'

Jake looked round and saw a fair-haired young man running over to them, red-faced from the sun. He said a few words to Sophie then called across to her companion, who was still watching the cubs from the other side of the enclosure. 'We're ready to roll, Mr Masters.'

Masters? Jake had heard that name before. As the dark-haired man took off his cap and came towards them, Jake realized who he was. 'It's Brandon Masters!' he whispered in awe to Shani.

'Who's that?' she asked, wrinkling her nose.

'You haven't heard of Brandon Masters?' Jake said in amazement. 'He's only the biggest star in Hollywood! I've seen all his movies.'

Shani raised her eyebrows. 'Well, I haven't seen any,' she said. Then she grinned at Jake. 'There aren't exactly a lot of places where you can see movies in Sibiti, you know.'

Jake felt as if he'd been stung – but gently! He hadn't meant to sound as if he was bragging. 'Sorry, Shani,' he told her.

'That's OK,' said Shani. 'One day I'll take you to our local cinema. It's in Dar es Salaam.'

'That sounds like a good idea,' commented the handsome actor, drawing level with them.

Shani leaned against the gnarled trunk of the umbrella tree. 'Maybe I'll take you too,' she offered him breezily.

'OK. Let's make a deal,' suggested Brandon, taking off his sunglasses. 'You show me where the cinema is, and I'll pay for the tickets. I'm Brandon, by the way.' He smiled at them, showing perfect white teeth in his lightly tanned face.

Unlike Shani, who didn't seem at all overwhelmed, Jake could hardly believe that he was meeting such a famous star. 'This is Shani, and I'm Jake Berman,' he stammered.

'Berman? As in the Bermans who run the reserve?' queried Brandon.

Jake nodded. 'Rick Berman's my stepdad.'

'Well, aren't you lucky, living in Musabi!' exclaimed Brandon. 'I'd trade my apartment in California for a spot out here any day. Wanna swap?'

'No way!' Jake laughed. Then, in case he sounded rude, he added, 'But you could come and stay with us, if you wanted.'

Brandon smiled, his deep blue eyes twinkling with amusement. 'You never know, I might just take you up on that one day.'

'Come on, Brandon, let's take Marigold and Marmaduke over to the set,' Sophie called over. She went to open the gate, which was secured with a heavy padlock.

'I'll help you carry them,' clamoured Raquel, skipping up to the gate.

Sophie looked down at the little girl. 'Not right now, Raquel,' she said gently, turning the key in the lock. 'Remember what your daddy told you. They still need time to get to know us.'

'But they won't *ever* get to know me if I can't play with them,' Raquel objected, pushing at the gate as Sophie opened it.

'They're not pets, Raquel,' Sophie warned her.

Just then, Brandon stepped forward. 'Hey, Raquel,' he said, taking her hand. 'Did I ever tell you about the time a big lion nearly got me when I was on safari in Kenya?'

Raquel's eyes grew wide. 'No,' she breathed. 'What happened?'

Brandon led Raquel away from the gate. 'We were on a night drive and he charged our jeep when we were watching his pride eating a zebra. I thought he was going to jump in and eat *me*!'

While Brandon was talking, Sophie slipped into the enclosure, shutting the gate behind her. Hearing it rattle, the cubs looked round, their stubby ears pricked. Warily, they watched Sophie approaching them.

Jake remembered Rick's earlier comment about the cubs still being rather wild. 'I wonder if they'll let Sophie pick them up?' he remarked to Shani.

Shani shrugged. 'Maybe they will if she's been feeding them.'

Sophie stopped a few metres from the little lions then crouched down and waited. 'Hi guys,' she said gently.

Marmaduke took a few cautious steps towards her. Marigold tagged along behind him then, with a sudden burst of confidence, trotted past him and stretched her neck towards Sophie's outstretched hand.

'Looks like Marmaduke's not as outgoing as his sister,' Jake whispered to Shani.

'Brothers never are,' she answered with a chuckle. Jake caught her eye and grinned. Shani had three older brothers and had no trouble keeping them in line!

Sophie took a few pieces of dried meat out of her pocket and offered them to the cubs. In a flash, Marmaduke bounded forward and grabbed the meat.

'Typical boy,' Shani laughed.

While Marmaduke gnawed on the meat, Sophie scooped him up and tucked him under one arm then leaned forward to pick up Marigold. But the little female scampered away playfully.

'She's playing hard to get,' Jake laughed.

'She loves a game, that's for sure,' Sophie remarked, hearing him. She stood up and carried Marmaduke over to the gate. 'Hold him for a minute please, Jake, while I get Marigold,' she said.

Almost before he knew it, Jake found himself with a surprisingly heavy lion cub in his arms. Marmaduke wrapped his front paws tightly around one of Jake's hands, while his thick fluffy tail swished from side to side, brushing against Jake's arm.

Jake gazed down at the young lion. Marmaduke looked back at him with huge amber eyes. 'You're awesome!' Jake murmured.

Shani reached across and stroked Marmaduke's soft coat. 'Poor boy,' she soothed.

Jake wrinkled his face at her. 'What do you mean? He's OK, isn't he? He looks strong and healthy.'

'Oh, sure,' replied Shani. 'And he'll grow even bigger and stronger. But I still feel really sorry for him.'

FIVE

'Why?' Jake couldn't understand why Shani was being so difficult about the cub.

Shani gazed at Jake, her brown eyes troubled. 'Because he'll be in America, and not in the African bush where he belongs.'

Marmaduke squirmed in Jake's arms, rubbing mud from his coat on to Jake's T-shirt. Jake could feel the cub's sinewy muscles flexing under the fur – muscles that in years to come would make him one of the most powerful animals on the African continent. He pictured Marmaduke as a huge, black-maned adult and in that moment, Jake understood what Shani meant. Keeping such a magnificent creature in captivity, especially in a foreign country, just didn't seem right. 'I guess you've got a point,' he admitted. 'Perhaps Marmaduke and Marigold should be allowed to stay in Africa.'

Shani only had time to nod because Raquel was suddenly at Jake's side, stretching up to grab Marmaduke's front paw. 'I want to hold him too,' she whined. 'Give him to me.'

'No, Raquel,' said Brandon, hurrying over. 'He might scratch you.'

'He won't, he won't,' chanted the child. 'He likes me, see?' She tried to touch the cub's face but before she could, Hank returned and took hold of her hand.

'You can see the cubs again later when they've finished their work,' he told her. 'It's time for your math lesson now. Your tutor's waiting for you.'

'I hate math,' Raquel grumbled. 'I want to play with my cubs.'

Hank took her by the shoulders and turned her to face the tented area. 'Listen, honey. If you go for your math lesson now, I'll ask Caron to do some shots of you and the cubs later.'

'For the movie?' Raquel asked, her eyes lighting up.

'Sure,' her father promised. 'So let's go and find your tutor.'

Pacified, Raquel set off with Hank, turning once to wave and call out to the cubs, 'See you later, Marigold and Marmaduke.'

'Right then. To work,' said Sophie, carrying Marigold out of the enclosure.

With Jake still holding Marmaduke, they went across to the film set. Halfway there, Sophie said, 'You'll be feeding the cubs during this scene, Brandon, so I just need to fetch a couple of their bottles from the kitchen tent.' She turned to Shani. 'Would you like to carry Marigold for me?'

'You bet!' replied Shani, her face lighting up as Sophie placed the furry bundle in her arms. But her smile quickly changed to a grimace when Marigold hooked the claws of one fluffy paw into Shani's hand. 'Ouch!' she exclaimed. With her free hand, she unhooked the razor-sharp claws. 'You don't have to hold on so tightly, Marigold,' she scolded gently. 'I won't drop you.'

Jake looked gratefully at Marmaduke's front paws which were folded softly around his hands.

'Shall I take Marigold back?' Sophie offered, looking concerned.

Shani shook her head. 'No, I'm OK.' Unruffled, she looked at her hand. 'She only made a few marks.'

'All the same, I'll bring you some antiseptic ointment,' said Sophie.

The film set was bustling with activity when Jake, Shani and Brandon arrived. The technical crew were positioning banks of lights, camera cranes and microphones all around the fake house, while the grips were putting items of furniture on the veranda.

Jake looked round. 'What's happening in this scene?' he asked Brandon.

'It's the opening scene,' Brandon explained. 'The character I'm playing is the owner of a ranch and I've recently taken in a pair of orphaned cubs. I'm also trying to impress a beautiful visitor to my farm, but the cubs keep creating mayhem.'

'That should be easy enough for Marmaduke and Marigold,' chuckled Shani.

A woman wearing a baseball cap hurried over to Brandon. 'I need to re-touch your make-up,' she told him. She led him away to a table and chair under a tree where she started applying powder to his face with a sponge.

'Make-up?' echoed Shani, wrinkling her nose at Jake. 'For a man?'

'I'm afraid so,' grinned Sophie, appearing behind them. She was holding two big babies' bottles filled with milk, as well as a tube of ointment for Shani. 'All the actors have to wear it.'

Jake saw Caron Lucas on the far side of the set, talking to the operator of a small machine that looked a bit like a generator. The operator flicked a switch, and at once wisps of smoke drifted out of the machine. Within minutes, the veranda and house were surrounded by very real-looking mist.

'That's amazing!' Jake breathed, half expecting to feel the cool dampness of early morning on his skin.

'It's a mineral oil burner,' explained Sophie. 'The smoke is non-toxic, so it's safe to breathe.'

With the mist swirling around the homestead, it was time for the cubs to make their first appearance.

'Ready, Brandon?' asked the producer.

Brandon made himself comfortable in a swinging couch and nodded to Sophie. 'OK, bring them on,' he grinned.

Sophie tried to take Marigold from Shani, but the cub hissed crossly and lashed out at Sophie with her claws.

'Sorry! Did I do something wrong?' Sophie murmured. She reached for Marigold again but the cub crouched back against Shani, her ears flattened.

Seeing his sister being so defensive, Marmaduke puffed himself up in Jake's arms and growled.

'Oh my,' laughed Sophie. 'Little prima donnas already – and you haven't even been in front of the cameras yet!'

Mr Alderton looked across at them, shading his eyes with his hand. 'Sophie,' he called out. 'We haven't got all day.'

'Coming, Hank,' replied Sophie. She smiled at Jake and Shani. 'You guys seem to have made friends with these two rascals pretty quickly! How about being my assistants for this scene?'

'You mean teach them tricks?' Jake asked cautiously. After being on the receiving end of the fly swat in the trading store, he agreed with Shani now when it came to the idea of performing lions.

'No. Nothing like that,' Sophie reassured him. 'In fact, we want the cubs to behave as naturally as possible. They need to create all sorts of realistic havoc. You just need to help me make sure they're in the right place at the right time, for each scene. And right now, this means carrying them over to the set.'

Staggering slightly under Marmaduke's weight, Jake followed Shani up the steps on to the veranda. Sophie gave Brandon the bottles of milk. 'Now let's see if the cubs will go to Brandon,' she said to Jake and Shani.

This time, the cubs didn't protest at finding themselves handed to someone else, even though it was a bit of a squeeze to fit them on to the swinging couch next to Brandon. Seeing the bottles in the actor's hands, the pair latched hungrily on to the rubber teats.

'Great!' called out Hank from his place next to the camera. 'Let's roll.'

Flashing an excited grin at Shani, Jake ran down the steps and went over to a shady spot in front of the veranda where they would have a good view of all the action. Sophie, meanwhile, kept out of sight behind the wooden façade, close enough to be able to give Brandon a hand with the cubs if necessary.

Jake rested his arms on a low-hanging branch of the tree as he watched Pete going to stand in front of Caron's camera with a clapperboard that bore the title of the movie. 'The Trouble with Lions, Take 1,' Jake read.

Mr Alderton signalled to Caron. 'Action!' he called.

Pete slammed shut the black and white striped bar on top of the clapperboard, then quickly ducked out of sight.

Looking relaxed, Brandon smiled down affectionately at the two cubs slurping away at the bottles. After a few seconds, a man dressed in a smart white suit came out of the front door, carrying a tray of tea. He put the tray on a side table next to Brandon.

'Thank you, Victor,' said Brandon.

The man nodded politely then left the veranda. Just then, a portable phone rang. It was on the table next to the tray. Brandon looked at the cubs then at the phone. He tried to pick it up but with his arms full of lion cubs, he eventually gave up and with a loud sigh said, 'You guys are really making life difficult around here.'

Mr Alderton stood up and shouted, 'Cut!' As the camera stopped rolling, he looked round at the crew, smiling. 'Perfect! Let's hope the rest of the lion scenes go that smoothly.'

'Thanks, guys,' smiled Brandon, stroking the cubs. 'You're great co-stars!' He tried to take away the bottles but the cubs sank their teeth into the teats and growled menacingly.

'Er, Sophie,' said Brandon, twisting his head round. 'I think I need your help here.'

Sophie hurried out and picked up Marmaduke, allowing him to keep the bottle in his mouth. Then she turned and beckoned to Jake. 'Could you take Marigold for me, please?'

Jake bounded up the wooden steps in three strides and carried the little female off the set behind Sophie.

Pete, meanwhile, had brought out a portable cage that looked like a baby's wooden playpen and was setting it up in the shade next to Shani.

'This is for the cubs between scenes,' Sophie explained to Jake, putting Marmaduke inside.

Jake put Marigold in with her brother then sat down next to Shani while the next scene was being set up. 'Isn't this great?' he said enthusiastically.

Shani reached a hand through the bars of the pen and tickled Marigold's tummy. 'Yes. And the cubs seem to be enjoying themselves, too!' The little cub grunted and twitched her belly.

Jake noticed a glamorous woman approaching the set. She was tall and willowy with gleaming golden hair, and she was wearing a spotless white safari suit.

'Who is she?' Jake asked Sophie, who was squatting beside him while she flicked through a copy of the film script.

'That's Felicia Ray,' answered Sophie, looking up. 'Also known as Mrs Hank Alderton.'

'So the whole Alderton family will have something to do with this movie,' commented Shani. 'Is Felicia as famous as Brandon?'

'Just about,' said Sophie with a grin.

The actress went up to Hank who put his arm round her and kissed her cheek. 'It looks like everything's going smoothly,' Felicia observed, looking round the set.

'So far, so good,' replied her husband.

From his seat on the veranda, Brandon smiled at Felicia. 'Hi, Felicia. All set for this scene? Our co-stars are real little professionals already! You'll love them.'

Felicia smiled faintly, and went to wait behind the façade ready for her cue. Hank signalled to Sophie to bring the cubs back on to the veranda.

'Could you give me a hand to get them out of here, please?' Sophie asked Jake and Shani.

'Sure,' said Jake, jumping up and dusting off his shorts.

Shani climbed inside the pen and picked up the cubs one by one then gave them to Jake and Sophie who carried them across to the set.

'We need to put them behind the sofa,' Sophie explained. 'The plan is for them to pop out and give Felicia's character a fright.'

But as they approached the sofa, Felicia suddenly looked out from behind the façade and peered at the cubs. With a look of horror on her face, she backed away, declaring loudly, 'Don't anyone bring those animals near me. They've got ticks.'

'Where?' asked Jake, craning his neck to look.

'There. On that one's ear,' said Felicia, pointing to Marigold with her mouth turned down in disgust.

Jake bent down to look closer. Sure enough, there

was a fat, grey tick attached to where the ear joined the cub's furry head.

'Sorry, Felicia,' said Sophie. 'I should have noticed that before.' She pulled off the parasite with a deft tug and squashed it under her foot. 'I guess out here in the bush, it would be a miracle if these little chaps didn't pick up a few ticks and fleas.'

Felicia turned pale. 'Fleas too!' she exclaimed. She looked across at her husband. 'I hope you don't expect me to touch these animals, Hank,' she warned.

'But, honey,' responded Hank, 'you know they're supposed to climb on to your lap when you're sitting down.'

'Then change the script!' demanded Felicia.

Hank groaned and shook his head. He picked up the script and studied it with a pen in his hand. Jake guessed he was looking for places to change the action. He couldn't help feeling a bit frustrated with Felicia's fussiness. Ticks and fleas were hardly life-threatening.

The little lions were wriggling energetically in Jake and Sophie's arms by now. 'Let's put them down,' Sophie suggested. 'But we'd better keep a close watch on them.' She glanced at Felicia who was sitting on a bench at the far end of the set, then beckoned to Shani to come and give a hand too. With a broad grin, Shani ran up the steps to join them.

Unrestrained, the cubs began to investigate the veranda, their noses to the floor and their tails held stiffly behind them. Within moments, they were heading towards Felicia.

'Hey, you rascals, come back here!' Jake scolded.

Felicia frowned, then went to sit with Hank, who was still making changes to the script.

'She's not taking any chances,' Shani murmured to Jake, her brown eyes sparkling with amusement.

'Yes. But I think it's going to be impossible to keep the cubs away from her,' Jake pointed out. Out of the corner of his eye, he saw Marmaduke pounce on a wire trailing across the floor. 'Watch out, you little monster!' he laughed, making a grab for the cub. He unravelled the wire from Marmaduke's paws then picked him up while a crew member taped the wire down safely.

Hank looked up and studied the veranda for a moment. 'I guess we can film the scene so it only *looks* as if the cubs are coming to you,' he said to Felicia. 'They can come out from behind the couch, then someone can lure them away from you in the other direction.'

Sophie suggested that the cubs' bottles of milk might be a good enough distraction. 'Jake and Shani could hide with the cubs and release them on cue. When they come out, I'll be just off camera, waving the bottles.'

'Cool,' said Jake to Shani. They squeezed behind the couch holding the wriggling cubs tightly.

'Not yet, Marmaduke,' Jake said, battling to keep him from escaping.

To make sure they couldn't be seen, Sophie draped a floor-length throw over the couch. Jake felt as if they were in a hot, stuffy tent. 'I wish they'd hurry up,' he muttered as Marmaduke writhed impatiently in his arms. His claws were razor sharp, and Jake could feel a stinging scratch on his right shin.

'Ssh,' whispered Shani, peeping out to see what was happening. 'Pete's got the clapperboard ready.'

They heard Hank shout, 'Camera. Action!' Then, as Felicia and Brandon came up the steps on to the veranda, Jake and Shani let go of the cubs and gave them a gentle push.

Their claws slipping on the smooth wood floor, Marmaduke and Marigold bundled out from under the cloth. They looked around but instead of running across the set, they began wrestling together, while

Brandon and Felicia waited in vain on the far side of the veranda.

'Cut!' shouted Mr Alderton. 'Let's try it again.'

This time, the cubs went bounding across the floor straight for Felicia, ignoring Sophie's frantic waving with the bottles.

Felicia gasped. 'Get them away from me!' she ordered, ducking behind Brandon.

'Cut!' shouted Mr Alderton again and Jake and Shani went charging after the cubs. Jake glanced enviously at the bottle of water one of the crew had just handed to Felicia. He was roasting under the artificial lights, and his throat felt dry as dust. Filming definitely wasn't glamorous or easy!

'Take Three,' announced Hank. On cue, Jake and Shani let the cubs go and this time, instead of heading for Felicia, they skidded off to one side and shot across the veranda, towards a flock of guineafowl that had been scratching for food on the ground. With feathers flying, the large blue-faced birds scattered, some running away at top speed while others flapped heavily up into the trees, cackling.

'Cut!' called Hank again, mopping his brow and looking exasperated.

Jake and Shani tore off to retrieve the cubs. When they brought them back on to the veranda, they caught Brandon's eye and the actor began to roar with laughter. Next to him, Sophie looked very amused, while down in front Hank was smiling broadly too. Even Felicia seemed to see the funny side. She shook her head and smiled, then went to sit with her husband while Jake and Shani positioned themselves behind the sofa yet again, each with a wriggling armful of cub.

From under the cloth Jake heard Hank ask Sophie if she had any other ideas. 'At this rate we'll be here for ever,' he said.

'We need a lure they can't resist,' said Sophie.

'Like the guineafowls?' Hank joked.

'That sort of thing,' answered Sophie. 'But I don't think the birds will co-operate.'

Jake had a sudden idea. He poked his head out from under the cloth. 'What if we get a bunch of guineafowl feathers and tie them together?' he called to Hank and Sophie. 'We can drag that across the ground in front of the cubs.'

Hank nodded. 'Makes sense to me,' he said. 'Let's give it a go.'

While Sophie and Brandon held the cubs, Jake and Shani quickly gathered a pile of the long spotted feathers then tied them together at one end of a long rope which Pete found for them.

'Let's get the cubs interested before we start shooting,' suggested Sophie.

'OK,' said Jake. He uncoiled the rope and dragged the feathers across the ground past the cubs who were sitting next to Sophie and Brandon on the veranda. As the feathery creature skimmed away from them, they jumped up and hurled themselves after it.

'No, you don't. Not yet,' Jake warned, pulling the lure out of their reach and hiding it behind his back.

'Well done, Jake,' called Hank. 'OK, guys, let's get cracking. Sophie, Shani, you take the cubs behind the sofa. Jake, you wait there with the lure. And, action!'

The fourth take was perfect. The cubs shot across the floor after the feathered lure and Felicia was able to deliver her lines while Jake kept Marmaduke and Marigold well away from her. Everyone looked enormously relieved when Mr Alderton finally called out, 'Cut! It's a wrap,' then announced it was time for lunch.

Sophie told Jake and Shani that the cubs would not be needed again that day so they took them back to their enclosure. On the way there, Sophie asked the two friends if they'd be able to come back in the morning. 'Just in case we need you – or your cool ideas – again,' she smiled.

Jake didn't hesitate. He didn't care how hot and thirsty he was now. Not everyone had the chance to be involved in a real movie! 'We'll be here first thing,' he promised.

It was lunchtime for the cubs, too, so Jake and Shani waited with them in the enclosure while Sophie went to fetch some more milk. Tired after their busy morning, the little lions flopped down in the shade and went to sleep.

Jake stretched out in the grass near them and watched a flock of vultures soaring on the midday thermals. Shani sat chewing a grass stalk at his side while she studied a column of ants winding their way up a tree trunk. In the searing heat and stillness, Jake felt his eyelids growing heavy. He sat up and shook his head then went out of the enclosure and looked round the shade cloth to see if Sophie was coming yet. There was no sign of her but Jake noticed two men dressed in khaki safari clothes talking to Mr Alderton outside his tent. 'I wonder who they are?' he asked, turning to Shani and nodding his head towards the strangers.

Shani came over and followed his gaze. 'Maybe they're actors,' she guessed. 'They look a bit familiar.'

'Hang on,' Jake said, suddenly. 'Aren't they the

men who were in the shop the other day? The ones who sold the cubs to Sophie?'

'That's it!' said Shani. 'Russell Lawson and Lyle Havers. I wonder what they're doing here?'

'Probably checking on the cubs to make sure they're OK,' Jake said. He looked over his shoulder at the sleeping pair. 'Perfect timing, too. They couldn't be more relaxed!'

The two friends waited. Jake's stomach rumbled, and he hoped the men would come over soon so he could go and have some lunch. But Havers and Lawson didn't even glance across at the enclosure. Instead, they finished talking to Mr Alderton, shook his hand and strode over to their pick-up which was parked near the other vehicles. Without even a backward look, they drove away.

'That's odd,' Jake said, frowning. 'You'd think they'd want to see the cubs.'

'Maybe Mr Alderton told them the cubs were doing fine,' suggested Shani.

When Sophie returned with the milk and heard that Havers and Lawson had been to the camp without visiting the cubs, she was equally mystified. 'Like Shani says, they must have been happy to just take Hank's word that they're OK,' she said, giving the bottles to Jake and Shani.

Jake opened the gate and they went inside. He sat down next to Marigold and waved the bottle in front of her nose. The cub grabbed on to the teat and began to feed. Shani sat down next to them and pulled the still lethargic Marmaduke on to her lap. Without even opening his eyes, he latched on to the bottle, his fluffy cheeks working as he drank.

With their bellies full, the contented cubs rolled on to their backs in the grass and were quickly asleep again. Jake grinned to himself. Not much sign of the lean, mean hunters of the savanna now!

'Our turn now,' said Sophie, leading the way out of the enclosure to the crew's lunch that was spread out on a long table under the fever trees.

Hank was sitting at the top of the table. He poured himself a glass of wine and raised it in a toast. 'To the movie, and the hunt,' he announced.

'The hunt?' Sophie echoed, looking puzzled.

'Yes,' beamed the producer. 'I'm going on a hunting safari later this week. It's all arranged.'

Jake and Shani exchanged concerned looks. Jake knew that Rick didn't allow any hunting in Musabi.

'Where, dear?' asked Felicia, peeling a banana.

'Oh, next door,' Hank replied. 'In, er – what's the name of the place?'

'Kasaba?' Jake ventured.

'That's it,' said Hank, nodding.

'But Kasaba's a game reserve, like Musabi.' Shani frowned. 'People can't shoot animals in reserves.'

'Actually, they can,' Hank replied confidently. 'In Kasaba, there's a fee of a thousand dollars, which my contacts tell me will go a long way towards running the reserve.'

'A thousand dollars!' Felicia exclaimed. 'That's rather steep. What if you don't get anything?'

'Oh, I will,' Hank reassured her. He sipped his wine. 'You see, Havers and Lawson have just been to tell me they've identified a target. An old lioness. She's a loner and pretty much on her way out anyway, so they say.'

Jake could hardly believe he was hearing this. Beside him, he could feel Shani sitting rigid with horror.

How could anyone think of shooting a lioness?

SIX

Early the next morning, Rick dropped Jake and Shani at the camp before heading off to Chozi again.

'*Jambo! Habari?*' Jake greeted the askari who was patrolling the parking area, his gun in one hand.

The guard looked at them with wide eyes. '*Simba!*' he said solemnly.

'Lion?' Jake said. 'Have the cubs been up to more trouble?'

The askari shook his head. 'Not the cubs. *Simba jike!* Here in the camp.'

Jake whistled softly. Often, while lying awake in bed at night, he heard the repeated low rumblings of lions, an awesome sound that travelled for miles. The distant calls always sent a shiver down Jake's spine, so to have a lioness coming that close must have been something else altogether! 'Let's find out what happened,' he urged Shani, setting off at a run.

In the camp, the actors and crew were still shocked by what had happened. They stood around in small groups, talking animatedly about the lioness's visit. Felicia sat close to her tent, holding Raquel's hand tightly, and glancing every now and then at the three askaris patrolling the site.

Even Hank looked agitated. 'Is your father here?' he asked Jake at once.

Jake shook his head. 'He's gone to Chozi again. But he'll be back early this afternoon.'

'Well, be sure to tell him I want to speak to him,' said the producer, a deep frown creasing his forehead. 'I'll need to hire more guards.'

Sophie and Brandon came over, carrying trays of coffee. Brandon gave a mug to Hank then offered the tray to Jake and Shani.

'No thanks,' said Jake, screwing up his face. He fished in his rucksack for a carton of juice instead. Shani accepted the coffee and added four heaped spoons of sugar to it.

'I take it you've heard all about our nocturnal visitor,' said Sophie.

'Only that a lioness came into camp,' Jake said. 'Did you see her?'

'No,' said Sophie. 'But I certainly heard her.'

'Me too,' said Brandon, grimly. 'She sounded really close.'

'Did she do any damage?' asked Shani, taking a big gulp of coffee.

'Not to any of the tents, luckily,' said Brandon. He exchanged a quick glance with Sophie. 'But she did have a go at the cubs' enclosure.'

'What?' Jake gasped, a chill running down his spine as he suddenly realized how defenceless the cubs were, alone on the far side of the camp. 'Are they OK?'

'Yes. But come and see what she did to the fence,' urged Sophie, beckoning them across the camp site.

Jake followed her round the shade cloth and was shocked to see the damage. The strong wire fence was buckled and the gate so badly twisted it looked as if it could come off its hinges at any moment.

'The cubs must have been petrified,' Jake gasped. He scanned the enclosure and felt a pang of alarm when he couldn't see them. Then he spotted a familiar black-tipped tail sticking out from under a dense bush and sighed with relief. The cubs seemed to be sleeping off the terror of the night.

'Apparently they were very upset, squealing and running up and down,' said Sophie. 'Luckily though, two of the guards heard the lioness tearing at the fence. They ran across and fired into the air to chase her away.'

Hank had come over to the wrecked pen while Sophie was talking. 'They should have shot her,' he said grimly. 'We can't have wild animals jeopardizing the safety of the crew – or the cubs.' He beckoned to the tall askari who was standing watch a few metres from the enclosure. 'Any sign of the lion again?'

'No, *bwana*,' replied the man. 'She won't come now. She'll wait for dark and then she'll come back. Maybe this is her territory,' he made a sweeping gesture at the surrounding bush, 'and she is angry with the cubs because they're not from her own pride. Last night, it sounded like she wanted to kill them.'

'Well, that's not going to happen. So be sure and let me know if you see her,' Hank told the askari. 'Perhaps you should even patrol the riverbank? She could be waiting down there, in the shade.'

'OK, *bwana*,' said the guard, walking away from the enclosure.

Hank took off his panama hat and wiped away the sweat on his forehead. 'In the meantime, we'd better get this fence fixed,' he said to Sophie.

Raquel came hurtling round the shade cloth. 'Are my lions all right?' she demanded.

'Marigold and Marmaduke are fine,' Jake assured her. 'Look, they're under that bush, sleeping.' He pointed to the stubby twitching tail.

'Mommy, I want to go in and see them,' Raquel declared to Felicia who had followed her over.

'Not now,' Felicia told her shortly. 'Let's go back to the tents.'

'But Marigold and Marmaduke haven't got an askari to look after them,' Raquel said anxiously. 'What if the nasty lion comes back and hurts them?'

Hank put a comforting hand on her arm. 'She won't, honey,' he assured her. 'The guards know lots about wild animals, and they say the lioness won't come back until after dark. And we're going to make the cubs' cage much stronger so that not even the fiercest lion can get in.'

Raquel looked satisfied with this. 'OK, Daddy,' she said. She took hold of Felicia's outstretched hand and followed her mum back to the tents.

'Right,' said Sophie. 'Let's get this fence mended. Pete and I will go into Sibiti to pick up some more wire. Jake, Shani, the cubs aren't needed on set for a while, but you're welcome to hang out and watch the rest of the filming. We'll be back in a couple of hours, and we could use your help with the fence, if that's OK.'

Jake was only too glad to help make the cubs safer. 'Sure, Sophie. See you later,' he said, then he and Shani wandered over to the fever tree where they had sat before. 'I hope the filming will be as much fun as it was yesterday,' Jake said to Shani as they settled down in the shade.

'At least it should be easier without the cubs,' Shani joked.

Today's scene involved a quarrel between Victor, Brandon's cook, and Felicia, who had caused mayhem in the kitchen when she tried to bake a cake. There were loads of stops and starts with long pauses in between as the actors and Hank tried to get the tricky scene spot-on.

Jake hadn't realized that film-making could be so tedious. After he and Shani had been watching for nearly an hour, he gave up and sprawled out on his back with his eyes shut. 'I'm falling asleep,' he whispered to Shani.

'I know, it's really boring,' Shani agreed, stifling a yawn. 'Let's do something else.'

'We could go and see Marigold and Marmaduke,' Jake suggested, sitting up and running his hand through his hair. 'They might be awake now.'

'And even if they aren't, they'll still be more fun to watch than this bunch,' Shani said, with an indifferent glance at the actors on the set.

They slipped quietly away towards the shade cloth and were almost there when an anguished scream broke out from the direction of the enclosure. This was followed by loud snarls and another ear-piercing shriek.

'The cubs!' Jake yelled, feeling the blood drain from his face.

'*Simba jike!*' Shani exclaimed. 'She's come back.'

Jake broke into a run. But when he rounded the shade cloth, he could hardly believe his eyes. The two cubs were anything but helpless. Growling angrily and swiping at her with their claws outstretched, the two little lions had backed Raquel against the fence, and the girl looked utterly terrified.

SEVEN

'Don't move, Raquel!' Jake shouted. There was no time to use the gate. He ran straight to the fence and clambered up the wire then leaped down to the other side, landing squarely on his feet.

'Help!' screamed Raquel, burying her head in her arms as the cubs lashed out at her again. 'Take them away!'

Jake paused, frantically trying to think of what he could do. Suddenly he remembered the guineafowl feathers, which were still in his pocket.

'Hang on, Raquel,' he called, pulling out the feathers. *This had better work*, he prayed, charging across the enclosure. Just centimetres from the angry cubs, he stopped and clapped his hands loudly. Startled, the lions spun round, hissing menacingly and lashing out in self-defence. Jake felt a sharp jolt of pain as Marigold's claws raked his shin. He jumped back, clenching his teeth, but managed to drop the feathery lure in front of the cub's narrowed amber eyes.

The little female snapped at it and struck out with her paws with lightning speed. Matching her for swiftness, Jake swung the lure away from her and past Marmaduke, who reacted with the same split-second reflex. Now both cubs were watching him, their sides heaving and their fur standing on end.

'Catch it!' Jake urged, letting the bunch of feathers drop to the ground, then dragging it along with a jerking motion.

The cubs couldn't resist the new, moving prey. They zigzagged after it, pouncing over and over again. Jake concentrated hard. He couldn't let them catch the lure too soon. He had to get as much distance as possible between them and Raquel.

Out of the corner of his eye he saw Shani climb into the enclosure and hurry over to Raquel. He heard her comforting the little girl before helping her to her feet and over the buckled gate to safety.

With Raquel out of danger, Jake let go of the feathers. 'OK, it's yours now,' he said to the cubs.

With excited growls, the pair set upon their trophy, ferociously tearing at it until the bundle of feathers disintegrated.

Outside the enclosure, Shani had her arm round the shaken little girl. 'Calm down, Raquel,' she soothed.

'I was so frightened,' wailed Raquel, clinging to Shani.

'What were you doing in there anyway?' Shani asked as Jake hoisted himself over the fence and landed next to them.

'I just wanted to see if my cubs were OK,' whimpered Raquel. 'I was worried about them.'

'Oh, Raquel, don't you understand?' Shani exclaimed. She dropped her arm and shoved her hands into her pockets in frustration. 'Lion cubs aren't pets! They're wild animals.'

Raquel sniffed then stared at the scratches on her arms and legs. 'Look what they did to me,' she said, her face crumpling as fresh tears welled up in her eyes.

Jake couldn't help feeling a bit sorry for her, but he shared Shani's exasperation. Now, more than ever, he could see what Shani meant about lions belonging in the wild. 'It could have been a lot worse,' he pointed out.

Raquel stared at him for a moment, wide-eyed, then took a deep, shaky breath. 'Please don't tell my mom and dad,' she said. 'They'll be really mad, and they won't let me take the cubs home.'

'That wouldn't be a bad thing,' muttered Shani.

Jake couldn't have agreed more.

Raquel gave them a pleading look. 'You mustn't tell them,' she insisted. 'I promise I won't go in the enclosure on my own ever again.'

Jake thought for a moment. 'We won't say anything,' he said at last. Beside him, Shani raised her eyebrows, but Jake shook his head briefly to stop her from saying anything. He didn't think Raquel should be allowed to take the cubs home, but he was worried about Marmaduke and Marigold. If Raquel's parents found out what had happened, the cubs might end up in trouble – not Raquel.

'How are you going to explain all those scratches?' asked Shani.

Raquel shrugged and hung her head. 'I guess I could say I tripped and fell into a spiky bush.'

'Mmm. You might just get away with it,' said Shani, examining the claw marks. 'Come on, we'd better make sure they don't get infected.' She put her hand in her shorts' pocket and pulled out the tube of antiseptic ointment that Sophie had given her yesterday.

Jake laughed. 'Just as well we both came armed with cub-fighting equipment today.'

Shani took Raquel's hand and led her over to the bathroom tent where she washed the little girl's scratches before gently smearing the ointment on to them.

'Ouch! That stings,' complained Raquel.

'It would be stinging a lot more if Jake hadn't rescued you,' Shani told her firmly.

'You sound like a bossy nurse!' Jake grinned at Shani.

'Well, don't forget who my mother is,' replied Shani. She looked at the angry red mark that Marigold had left on Jake's shin. 'I think you'd better use some of this too,' she said, tossing the tube to him.

Jake pushed aside the mosquito net that surrounded the big iron bath in the middle of the tent and sat down on the rim. The bath had four claw-shaped feet, and reminded Jake of the tub in his gran's cottage in England. Only in Oxford there were no mosquito nets! 'By the way,' he said to Raquel, 'what did you do to make the cubs so cross?'

Raquel hesitated and looked at the ground. 'We were playing tag,' she said in a small voice. 'I showed them some of that dry meat that Sophie gave them the other day. Then I ran away to make them chase me.'

'Big mistake!' said Shani. 'You should have let them have the meat.'

'And if you run away from lions – even small ones – they'll always attack you,' Jake put in, remembering Rick's advice.

'I didn't know that,' muttered Raquel. 'I thought they liked playing tag, like my puppy at home.'

Jake felt a knot of frustration. He wanted to go straight to Mr Alderton to tell him what had happened. But he couldn't help suspecting that Hank Alderton would blame the cubs, not his daughter's daft ideas. *We'll just stick with the first plan*, Jake decided, *and cover up the whole thing. At least Raquel might have learned a lesson from it.*

With her wounds cleaned and her face washed, Raquel seemed calm enough to have her morning lessons. Jake and Shani watched her go into the tent where her tutor was waiting, then they went back to the cubs' enclosure. The sun was now almost at its peak, and with not a breath of wind in the air, the cruel dry heat burned down ruthlessly upon the camp. Jake pulled his baseball cap further over his eyes to keep out the glare.

Inside their enclosure, Marmaduke and Marigold seemed to have forgotten all about the scrap with Raquel. They lay sprawled out side by side, their legs and tails entwined, twitching their ears and whiskers to chase away the flies that were trying to settle on their faces.

Jake and Shani sat on the ground and leaned against a rock in the shade. Jake was soon feeling restless and sticky. Not far away, the shrunken river that divided Musabi from the Kasaba game reserve sparkled invitingly. 'I'd do anything for a swim,' he said, looking longingly at a section where the water cascaded over some smooth rocks.

'Well, I'm not stopping you,' grinned Shani. 'Go ahead. I'll stay here and watch you.'

'Watch me vanish, you mean?' Jake laughed. He knew just how risky it would be to go in the river. Even though the water was mostly very shallow, danger lurked in the form of crocodiles sunning themselves on the mud flats on the Kasaba side of the river, while hippos wallowed almost unseen in the deeper pools.

Jake sighed and began to mark out a noughts and crosses grid in the dust next to him. He drew a cross in the middle square and just as Shani placed a nought above it, Sophie, Brandon and two crew members – Pete and Yani – appeared round the shade cloth with a new gate and a roll of wire mesh.

'Well, these two rascals look pretty relaxed,' said Sophie, seeing the cubs asleep. 'You'd never guess they'd had a scary experience last night.'

And this morning, Jake wanted to add as he and Shani jumped up and went round to the gate.

Sophie had brought the cubs' lunch bottles with her so she and Shani fed the pair, while Jake gave Pete and Yani a hand with the new gate.

'Makes a nice change from acting,' joked Brandon, opening a box of tools and selecting a pair of pliers.

Jake and Brandon removed the twisted gate then held the new one in place while Pete and Yani bolted it to the post. Next, they covered the torn sections of the fence with strong wire mesh.

When the repairs were completed, Brandon stood back to admire the team's handiwork. 'Not bad, even if I do say so myself,' he said. 'That should keep out any intruders.'

'Let's see if there's any lunch left for us,' said Sophie, coming out of the enclosure with Shani and leaving the satisfied cubs to sleep off their meal in the shade.

'There had better be,' said Brandon, handing the pliers to Yani who was packing up the toolbox. 'I'm ravenous.'

On the way to the lunch table, Jake noticed Hank talking to two men in the parking area. 'Havers and Lawson again,' he said aloud, recognizing them at once.

'Come to finalize arrangements for the hunt, no doubt,' Sophie suggested.

Jake clenched his fists with silent anger. It looked like nothing could be done to save the targeted lioness. Last night at home, he had told his mum and Rick about the producer's plan. They were both just as troubled about it as he was. But Rick explained that controlled hunting was indeed legal and that several game parks, like Kasaba, used it to raise funds. Jake was glad that Musabi was different.

Havers and Lawson drove away and Hank joined everyone for lunch. He seemed more cheerful than ever as he sat down and reached for a can of iced beer. 'Hey, guys, I've had some extraordinary news,' he announced.

'What about?' asked Felicia, fanning herself with her script.

'I told Lyle and Russell about the attack last night,' said her husband. 'They wanted to know if anyone had seen the lioness. So I called the askaris, and they told me they'd noticed a long scar on her shoulder.'

'What's so interesting about a scar?' said Felicia, examining her scarlet nails. Jake thought she seemed bored with the subject of the lioness now that the immediate danger had passed.

'The point, honey,' Hank told his wife patiently, 'is that the scar identifies thc trespassing lioness as . . .' he paused and looked around the long table, '. . . the same animal I'll be hunting tomorrow!'

EIGHT

A hum of amazement sped round the table. 'Is it just a coincidence that she came here?' asked Pete. 'Or does she suspect that something's up?'

'That's it!' laughed someone else. 'She was trying to find you, Hank, before you found her.'

'Well, if that's what she was after, she came right into the lion's den!' retorted Hank, his eyes twinkling with amusement. 'I'll be ready for her if she comes back again.' He raised his arms as if he was holding a rifle, and mimed a shooting action.

Jake was astonished. He couldn't believe that Hank intended to shoot the lioness right here in the camp! He took a deep breath. 'Er, my dad doesn't allow shooting at Musabi,' he began hesitantly.

'Well, this is a very unusual situation,' the producer pointed out. 'As I understand it, the lioness belongs to Kasaba, so technically speaking, she's mine. I'm sure Havers and Lawson will confirm that when they come round later.'

Jake didn't want to get into an argument, but he mentally crossed his fingers that Rick would be able to do something to protect the lioness. Throughout lunch, he kept an eye open for the Land Rover. As soon as he saw it winding its way down the road to the site, he excused himself from the table and ran to meet it in the parking area.

Shani raced over with him. 'Your dad's got to stop Mr Alderton,' she puffed.

'He will,' Jake said confidently.

Rick was surprised to find them waiting for him. 'I thought I'd have to tear you away from those cubs,' he smiled, pulling up next to them.

Jake was tempted to tell Rick how he had had to tear the cubs away quite literally from Raquel, but he decided that particular news could wait. Right now there was something more pressing Rick needed to know. 'Mr Alderton's planning to shoot a lioness tonight, here in the camp,' he blurted out.

'What?' asked Rick, frowning.

Jake quickly told Rick about the incident in camp during the night.

Rick was clearly very troubled about the lioness's visit and particularly about her attack on the cubs. 'That's pretty strange behaviour,' he said shaking his head slowly when Jake finished his account.

'Yes, but the worst thing is that Mr Alderton has sent a message to Kasaba for Havers and Lawson to come back later to help him shoot the lioness,' Jake added.

Rick took off his sunglasses and swung himself out of the Land Rover. 'There'll be no shooting here, not unless it's a life-or-death situation. I'll send more askaris to patrol the camp, though.' He pushed back his broad-brimmed hat and strode purposefully over to Hank.

Feeling very relieved, Jake followed him. 'I told you Rick would sort it out,' he murmured to Shani.

Hank greeted Rick warmly. 'Hi,' he said, getting up to shake Rick's hand. 'The very man I want to speak to.'

'Sorry to hear about the lioness last night,' said Rick, coming straight to the point. 'I'll send an extra team of guards down here right away.'

'No need!' said Hank confidently. 'I'll be on guard myself, with Russell and Lyle.'

'Well, that's a whole different ball game,' said Rick calmly. 'You see, we don't shoot animals at Musabi, unless it's unavoidable.'

'Oh, but it *is* unavoidable in this case,' Hank assured him. 'I mean, people's lives are at stake, not to mention the cubs.'

Rick stood his ground. 'Mr Alderton, I'm responsible for the safety of people in this park,' he said. 'So I decide on what measures to take if, and when, there's danger. In this case, more guards are needed. They're quite capable of dealing with this sort of thing.'

'You wouldn't think so,' retorted Hank scornfully. 'Your guys didn't know the lioness was here until she'd nearly killed the cubs.'

'A lioness could be a few metres away and you wouldn't know it,' Rick told him, defending his men. 'And, believe me, if she'd come anywhere near the tents, the askaris would have seen her. You were all safe enough.'

'How do we know she wasn't prowling around the tents?' Hank argued, looking rather red in the face.

'That's easy enough to find out,' Rick countered. 'We can look for her tracks.'

'Great idea!' Jake exclaimed. He wished he'd thought of that this morning. He had begun to learn about tracking animal spoors during bush walks with Rick and Morgan, Shani's uncle. Already, he could identify the prints of rhinos, zebras, lions, antelope and hyenas.

'OK. Let's have a look then,' agreed Hank.

They went across to the tents and began to scrutinize the dusty ground for signs of the lioness. Jake glanced every now and then at Hank. The producer was peering at the ground as if he wasn't too sure of what he was looking for.

Jake studied the soft soil around his boots. There were dozens of prints, all of them made by human feet. A few others, some distance from the tents, told of some non-human visitors – monkeys, antelope and guineafowls.

Suddenly Hank bent down and patted the ground. 'Here! Have a look at this,' he announced triumphantly.

Jake sprinted over to him and looked at the trail of stubby paw prints. 'I don't think that's lion spoor,' he ventured, just as Rick joined them. He looked up at his stepdad. 'Do you?'

Rick examined the prints and an amused look crossed his face. 'Nothing to worry about here, Hank,' he said. 'A lone jackal made these. He won't do you any harm.'

They continued to search the area around the tents. Jake found more jackal prints, and Shani found the telling zigzag trail of a snake in deep sand. But there was not a single feline paw mark.

At last, Rick took off his hat and ran his hand through his hair. 'Not a trace of the lioness. If she'd been here, I'd have found the prints,' he promised. 'You weren't on her agenda, Hank.'

'OK. But that just shows it was no accident she went for the cubs,' Hank insisted. 'So she'll be back to finish them off. And then, who knows, she might even have a go at us. I need to make sure the cubs and my team will be safe.'

'You can do that by trusting me and the askaris to do our job,' Rick said coolly.

Hank folded his arms meaningfully. 'You're forgetting one thing,' he said. 'The lion's mine. I've already paid the money. If I shoot her here or in Kasaba, it's all the same.'

Jake felt deflated. Mr Alderton seemed to have all the answers! He shot Rick an appealing look. His stepdad *had* to find a way of stopping Hank.

But before Rick could speak, Felicia came out of her tent. She saw Rick and flashed him a dazzling smile. 'Have you come to protect us all from danger?' she teased.

'That's right, Mrs Alderton,' Rick said in a matter-of-fact tone. 'There'll be no more trouble.'

'You bet!' exclaimed Hank, putting his arm round Felicia and winking at Raquel, who had followed her mother out. 'And if anyone's going to be doing the protecting, it's me. Just think, honey,' he told his wife proudly, 'I'll be bagging one terrific trophy.'

'I hope you're not planning on taking the body home,' Felicia said bluntly.

'Of course I am,' answered Hank, looking surprised. 'I've got to have the evidence. The pelt will look great on the wall of my study.'

Felicia clearly wasn't impressed. 'I don't think so, Hank,' she said. 'I'm not having any dead animals stuck on walls in my home. A photograph will be proof enough.' She shook off Hank's arm and headed for the film set. 'Come on, Raquel. It's time to shoot your scene.'

Rick was looking thoughtful. 'Do you mind if I check the enclosure, Hank?' he asked.

'Be my guest,' Hank said generously, obviously confident he had won the debate. 'I'll come along too. I was going to look at the repairs anyway.'

They went across to the enclosure where the cubs were still asleep. Hearing them approach, Marigold lifted her head lazily and glanced at them before rolling over to resume her siesta.

Rick examined the fence, then studied the ground and pointed out the lioness's trail. Jake spotted the prints easily, like huge versions of a pet cat's paw marks.

'Let's see which way she went,' said Rick, following the trail down the slope towards the river. A few metres on, he stopped. 'It looks like she definitely came from Kasaba,' he said, shielding his eyes with one hand and looking across to the neighbouring reserve.

Hank nodded approvingly. 'Just like I said,' he agreed.

Jake and Shani exchanged looks of alarm. Everything seemed to be going the producer's way.

'The thing is,' continued Rick, coming back up the slope, 'I'm not so interested in where the lioness came from, more in what she's up to. You see, something doesn't add up here.' He crouched down next to the fence and stared at the ground.

'What do you mean?' asked Hank, bending down next to him.

'First of all, if the lioness came from somewhere across the river, she couldn't have been behaving territorially,' Rick began.

Of course! Jake thought. Why would a lioness bother to come all the way over here to threaten cubs that weren't on her territory in the first place?

'And another thing,' continued Rick. 'Nothing points to the cubs being terrified. Quite the opposite, in fact.' He pointed out a host of paw prints, big outside the fence, smaller inside. 'It looks to me like all three animals spent a lot of time at the wire – not what you'd expect if the cubs felt threatened.'

'So she wasn't trying to kill them after all?' asked Shani.

Rick stood up. 'Probably not.'

'You can't prove that,' put in Hank. 'A bunch of prints is no reason for us to take any chances. I mean, if the lioness comes back and attacks someone, it'll look very bad for Musabi.'

'There'll be no attacking,' Rick said with authority. 'And there'll be no shooting tonight either – unless it's absolutely necessary. In which case, I'll be the one to do it.' He looked up at Hank. 'Mr Alderton, I'd like you to postpone your hunt for one more night. Something's going on here with this lioness, and I want to see what it is.'

Hank seemed rather surprised by Rick's request, but he agreed to give the lioness a second chance. 'I guess I can arrange to go to Kasaba later on this week,' he said, with a shrug. 'But what exactly are you planning to do?'

'I want to observe her,' Rick answered. 'I'll rig up a makeshift hide and spend the night there.' He turned to go. 'I'll collect all the equipment and be back before dusk. Come on, you two,' he said to Jake and Shani. 'You can help me load the stuff.'

Jake wanted to do more than just load things. He wanted to spend the night in the hide too, waiting for the lioness. He'd been on several night drives with Rick, and they'd seen lions almost every time, but he'd never camped out in the open, deliberately waiting for one to appear. As soon as he climbed into the Land Rover, he broached the subject. 'Can I join you in the hide?' he asked Rick.

'Me too!' said Shani eagerly.

'I was waiting for this,' sighed Rick.

'Please,' Jake begged.

'We won't get in the way,' promised Shani.

Rick started up the engine. 'I know,' he said. 'But it's dangerous. The lioness could be desperately hungry. She might even be sick or injured. You know that makes wild animals totally unpredictable.'

'You didn't say anything about that to Mr Alderton,' Jake argued, feeling the disappointment of Rick's almost certain refusal.

'Of course not. I needed to downplay the threat of danger. The man's trigger-happy enough already,' Rick retorted.

'But we're not,' Shani pointed out. 'And we wouldn't argue with you and the askaris. We'd keep right out of your way.'

Rick chuckled, then lapsed into silence as he steered the Land Rover up the dusty track out of the valley.

'Please, Rick,' Jake tried again. 'We've been in dangerous situations before. Like the time that elephant charged the Land Rover.'

'Ah. But I had my foot on the accelerator,' Rick reminded him.

'And this time, you'll have your finger on the trigger,' Jake argued.

Rick gave him a sideways look. 'It's easy to be flippant about it, Jake,' he said sternly. 'But being attacked by a lion is no laughing matter. And you should know.' He glanced down at the angry red scratch on Jake's leg. 'What happened?'

Jake swallowed. 'It was an accident . . .' he began.

'The truth, Jake,' Rick said firmly.

Jake took a deep breath then recounted the incident earlier that day. 'But don't worry, I don't think Raquel will bother the cubs again,' he added finally.

'You won't say anything to Mr Alderton, will you?' Shani pleaded with Rick.

'Too right, I won't,' he replied with unexpected firmness. 'Next thing, he'll want to finish off the cubs, too!'

They continued in silence for several kilometres but just after they rattled over the cattle grid at the entrance to the homestead, Rick pulled over and turned to look at Jake and Shani. 'We'd better phone your mum, Shani, to see if she's OK about you spending the night lion-watching,' he said.

Jake twisted round to grin at Shani. 'Great!' he said. 'Thanks, Rick. You won't regret it.'

Night was falling by the time the hide was ready back at the camp. It consisted of a wooden platform outside the enclosure, surrounded by green shade cloth and standing several metres high on a scaffold made from sturdy poles.

'Supper time,' Rick announced, hoisting himself up the scaffold. In his shirt pocket was a two-way radio keeping him in touch with the askaris posted to watch over the tents.

Jake and Shani climbed up behind Rick, then the three of them tucked into the picnic supplied by Mr Alderton's catering company.

In the enclosure, the cubs tumbled about. Something small scurried past them, its identity concealed by the long grass. The cubs picked up the movement in a flash and hurtled after the hidden creature as it scuttled away to the dense undergrowth on the other side of the fence. Thwarted, the cubs pawed at the wire a few times then gave up and returned to their sparring match.

The night grew darker. Among the tents, paraffin hurricane lamps lit up the site with a warm glow, and Jake picked out the figures of Sophie and Brandon sitting side by side on reclining camp chairs, their faces turned up towards the sky. Jake followed their gaze to the eastern horizon where the sky was darkest. It was peppered with the twinkling pinpoints of a trillion stars.

Gradually the sound of human conversation in the camp died down, giving way to the noises of the night. Crickets rubbed their hind legs together to signal to their mates, filling the air with their shrill monotonous theme. In stark contrast, Jake could hear the low croaking of a bullfrog choir gathered near the river.

An eerie double *whoop-whoop* followed by a peal of chortling laughter echoed from somewhere outside the camp. *'Fisi,'* whispered Shani, and Jake pictured a hyena loping through the savanna in search of a meal.

For two hours, the watchers in the hide waited. The cubs had long since fallen asleep and the only other sign of lions was the distant rumbling of a pride from deep inside Musabi. From Kasaba, there came nothing but silence.

Jake started to feel restless. 'It doesn't look like she's coming back tonight,' he sighed, opening the picnic basket in search of a snack.

'Patience,' Rick told him, his teeth flashing white as he smiled through the darkness.

Jake found a raw carrot and took a bite. The sharp *crunch* crackled in the still air like a rifle shot.

'Sssh!' hissed Shani. 'You'll scare everything away.'

Sheepishly, Jake put the rest of the carrot back in the basket. He peered out over the shade cloth, trying to see anything that might be of some interest.

Above them, a half moon hung in the velvet sky, covering the earth with a silvery blue light and casting strange shadows all around. But nothing stirred. Even the crickets and bullfrogs had fallen silent. And then, with no warning at all, the lioness appeared, a sleek, lean shape padding silently up the slope from the river. For the briefest moment,

Jake saw the amber glint of her eyes reflecting the moonshine as she looked his way.

Rick had seen her too. He glanced at Jake and Shani and put his finger to his lips, then leaned forward to watch.

The lioness moved purposefully along the same trail her prints had made the night before. In the moonlight, her coat was the colour of pale honey, flexing and creasing over her muscles as she made her way up the slope. At the top, she paused to look around. She was now only metres from the hide and Jake could see her face quite clearly. Scars from hunting and fighting criss-crossed her nose and forehead.

The lioness moved on again and Jake now saw that she was limping slightly. There was a jagged wound on her shoulder – a deep cut that was so fresh it hadn't yet healed properly. That was the mark that branded the lioness as Mr Alderton's victim! Jake pointed it out to Rick who nodded and mouthed silently, 'Fight wound, probably.'

The lioness was now less than an arm's length away from the hide, yet she made not a sound. No wonder the askaris hadn't seen her last night until it was almost too late. Jake could hardly breathe. He had never been so near to a fully-grown lion, and he felt suddenly vulnerable. How much protection were a few poles and a flimsy piece of netting against a hungry carnivore?

Out of the corner of his eye, Jake noticed Shani taking a step backwards as if trying to put some distance between herself and the dangerous big cat. As she did so, the wooden platform creaked loudly beneath them. The lioness froze. She pricked up her ears, listening for the unfamiliar noise again. In the hide, no one dared to move a muscle.

The lioness lifted her head and sniffed the air, her lower jaw dropping open to reveal her huge bottom canine teeth.

Could she smell them? In the heavy stillness, Jake could hear the blood pounding in his ears. The lioness wrinkled her nose and sniffed again then turned to look at the scaffold that supported the platform.

Jake went cold. The lioness knew they were there! Jake tore his eyes away for a moment to see what his stepdad was doing. But Rick was simply watching her, his hands not even on his rifle.

With a low, threatening rumble, the lioness padded towards them and disappeared from view under the platform. There was a thud from below, followed by an ominous tremor, as if the lioness was trying to climb the scaffold. Jake felt his head swim with terror. Then, to his utter relief, the mighty cat reappeared on the other side of the platform and padded away, the hide no longer of interest to her.

But now she was heading straight for the cubs' enclosure!

Jake's heart beat faster. In no way did the lioness fit the picture that Lawson and Havers had painted of a decrepit old creature nearing her end. Even though she was thin she was still a powerful and fearsome animal. And the fact that the wound was fresh showed she was still in fighting shape.

Jake glanced at the rifle hanging over Rick's shoulder. He hoped his stepdad wouldn't have to use it, but if the lioness meant to attack the cubs, the gun could be the only chance they had.

The lioness reached the fence. She padded alongside it, sniffing the ground, then suddenly dashed a huge front paw against the wire. The entire fence shook. The lioness pawed at it again, and Jake prayed silently that the repairs would hold. He also willed the cubs to stay asleep. He could just make them out, stretched out on the moonlit grass at the far side of the enclosure.

Just then, a mighty roar echoed through the night – the roar of another lion somewhere in Musabi. The lioness jumped and looked over her shoulder. She snarled loudly then spun round and threw her body against the wire, making it rattle violently.

The cubs woke up at once. They scrambled to their feet and looked around, mewling nervously. Outside, the lioness snarled again. She stood up on her hind legs and began tearing at the fence with her teeth.

The cubs cried louder, the high-pitched chirping sound almost drowned out by the adult's angry growls. And then, to Jake's despair, Marigold set off for the fence. Marmaduke watched her for a moment, head on one side, then he followed her, straight for the raging lioness.

'Stay where you are!' Jake hissed desperately. Beside him, Rick slipped the rifle off his shoulder.

When the lioness spotted the cubs, she threw herself at the fence with new strength, grabbing at the wire with her massive paws. The cubs stopped and stared at her, blinking in surprise.

In her frenzy, the lioness shoved a front leg through a gap in the wire, wrenching her shoulder so that the wound opened up and a steady stream of blood began to trickle down her flank.

Jake watched in horror. The lioness was going to kill the cubs!

NINE

The lioness pulled her leg back out of the fence and twisted her head round to lick her shoulder. In the sudden silence, the cubs looked briefly confused, then they trotted towards her again.

'We've got to stop them,' Shani cried.

Rick raised the rifle to his shoulder. 'Keep back, both of you,' he ordered Jake and Shani.

Shani grabbed Jake's arm and turned away. 'This is horrible,' she said in a choked voice.

Jake wanted to turn away too, but couldn't take his eyes from the scene below. He braced himself for the moment when the rifle cracked and Rick's well-aimed shot found its target.

But no shot blasted the night air. Instead, Rick slowly lowered his rifle. 'This isn't what we think it is,' he said quietly while in his shirt pocket, the two-way radio crackled to life.

'What's happening, *Bwana*?' came the voice of an askari. 'We can hear the lioness.'

'Yes. She's here. But everything's OK, Benjamin,' Rick whispered, then he slipped the radio back in to his pocket.

Jake gaped at Rick in amazement. 'What do you mean it's OK?' he croaked. As far as he was concerned, everything was *not* OK.

Down at the enclosure, the lioness was biting savagely at the wire again. On the other side, the cubs were pressing their bodies against the fence, mewling in agitation.

'I mean that the lioness doesn't want to harm the cubs,' Rick explained calmly. 'And they know it.'

'What?' gasped Shani. 'How can you tell?'

'By their body language,' answered Rick. 'It confirms my hunch this morning. The cubs aren't frightened – they're excited.'

'They can't be,' Jake exclaimed – but as he watched the three lions, he began to see what Rick meant. Padding back and forth next to the wire, just centimetres from the lioness on the other side, the cubs didn't look scared at all, with their ears pricked and their tails held high. 'They *are* excited,' Jake murmured, feeling his heart rate returning to normal.

107

'What's going on?' He reached for his night vision binoculars next to the picnic basket and focussed them on the lioness.

'Can I have a look?' Shani whispered.

'OK.' Jake was about to pass the binoculars to her when Marmaduke came into his view. 'Hey! Look at that!' he gasped, as the lioness paused in her frantic ripping at the wire to reach through and lick the cub's head. It was as close to a gesture of comfort as Jake could imagine. And then an idea came to him that only moments ago would have seemed quite crazy. 'Do you think she could be trying to get the cubs *out* of the enclosure?' he asked Rick quietly.

Rick narrowed his eyes and nodded. 'I was just wondering that myself,' he said, leaning his gun against one leg and raising his own binoculars. 'Because it seems to me that the cubs are pretty desperate to get to her.'

'Let me see,' said Shani, taking the binoculars from Jake.

Looking suddenly worn out, the lioness slumped on her side next to the fence, breathing heavily and licking the wound on her shoulder. Even without the binoculars, Jake could see her flinch. On the other side, meanwhile, the cubs ran back and forth, crying out with high-pitched yelps.

'Maybe they think she's their mother,' Shani suggested sadly, lowering the binoculars. 'They probably don't know a buffalo killed her.'

Rick looked thoughtfully at Shani then turned his attention back to the lions. After a while he said, 'You know what? I don't think a buffalo *did* kill their mother.'

'You don't?' Jake frowned.

Rick didn't take his gaze off the lions. 'I reckon she was just injured in the shoulder – like the one down there.'

'You mean . . .' Jake began, as an extraordinary idea took shape in his mind.

'Uh-huh,' Rick nodded. 'Incredible as it may seem, I think she's the cubs' mother.'

Jake stared at Rick, his mind racing. If the lioness was the cubs' mother, why had the Kasaba rangers said she'd been killed? How on earth did they get hold of the cubs if their mother was still alive?

Rick came up with some likely answers to Jake's unspoken questions. 'Look closely,' he said. 'You'll see the lioness is in milk. Proof that she's been nursing cubs very recently.'

Jake took the binoculars from Shani again and

focussed them on the lioness. She was still lying down, her eyes dull with pain and misery. For the first time, Jake noticed her swollen teats. 'But that doesn't *have* to mean she's their mother,' he pointed out. 'Maybe she lost her own cubs, and she wants to adopt Marmaduke and Marigold.'

Rick shook his head. 'I doubt it. A lioness will suckle cubs from her own pride, but she'd never seek out a pair not related to her.'

'So how did she know they were here?' asked Shani.

Rick shook his head. 'Who knows? Perhaps she came down to the river to drink and heard the cubs, then laid low until she thought it was safe to look for them.'

While Rick was talking, the lioness hauled herself up and began pounding the fence again. Copying her, the cubs stood up against the wire and struck it with their sturdy front legs.

'They're so desperate,' murmured Shani. 'I wish we could open the gate and let them out.'

'Out of the question,' Rick said firmly. 'If the lioness gets even the faintest hint that we're here, we'll be in more trouble than you know. She'll do anything to protect her cubs. So we stay put until she leaves at dawn when the camp starts waking up – *if* she leaves, that is.'

But the lioness showed no intention of leaving. She continued her steady bombardment of the enclosure, pausing only to draw breath and lick her wound from time to time.

'Why don't you phone Havers and Lawson tomorrow and ask them what really happened to the cubs' mother?' Jake whispered to Rick at one point.

Rick shook his head. 'I'm suspicious of those two and doubt we'd get the truth from them,' he said. 'I reckon they saw their chance to make some cash when they heard the movie company needed some cubs.'

'You mean they were lying when they told Sophie they'd rescued a pair of orphans?' Jake suggested. 'And then went to look deliberately for cubs?'

'Maybe,' Rick agreed. 'And it was just their luck to see the lioness being gouged by the buffalo. After all, they couldn't have stolen cubs from a healthy animal.'

'Yes. That wound must have slowed her up a lot,' remarked Shani, peering through the binoculars.

Rick nodded. 'Enough to stop her going back to her cubs for a day or two, for sure. Havers and

Lawson must have tracked them down and sold them to Sophie.'

'That's terrible!' exclaimed Shani.

'But now that the mother has found them, they can all go back to the bush,' Jake reasoned.

'That means they won't be going to America after all,' added Shani, throwing Jake a look of triumph.

Rick grimaced. 'I just hope it'll be that straightforward when it comes to sorting this out.'

'It will be,' Jake said with confidence.

Down at the enclosure the lioness was growing increasingly frustrated, padding around in a tight circle like a caged lion in a zoo. Suddenly she stopped and stared towards the tents.

'Now what?' whispered Rick as the lioness began to creep stealthily towards the camp, her ears pricked.

In a beam of moonlight, Jake saw what she was after. A single male warthog was grazing in the middle of the camp site, oblivious to the hungry lioness stalking him.

Jake heard Rick swear under his breath as he quickly shouldered his rifle. An ear-splitting crack shattered the peace as Rick fired into the air. The lioness whirled round, her eyes flashing with fear and anger, then fled, vanishing in an instant into the shadows. In the enclosure, the cubs stared into the darkness that had swallowed their mother up.

His ears ringing painfully, Jake looked up at his stepdad.

Rick took a deep breath and glanced down at Jake. 'Close,' he murmured, grimly.

Over in the camp, lights flickered on in the tents and Mr Alderton's voice boomed out. 'What happened? Did someone shoot the lion?'

'Come on, you two,' Rick said to Jake and Shani, double-checking that there were still bullets in the rifle before swinging himself over the side of the platform. 'We'd better go and tell him what happened. But stay close to me and keep watch, in case the lioness is still lurking near by.'

In the camp, Hank was standing just outside his tent, an askari at his side. Brandon jogged over from his tent, glancing cautiously over his shoulder.

'Why did you shoot?' Hank demanded when he saw Rick. 'I thought you said everything was OK?'

'The lioness was heading your way,' Rick explained as others emerged nervously from their tents.

'I knew it!' said the producer. He looked round at the assembled cast and crew. 'She means to attack us all. I should have shot her tonight like I planned to do.'

'She wasn't after any of you,' said Rick in a calm voice. 'She was going for a warthog.'

'And the cubs?' Sophie put in anxiously. 'Did the lioness go for them again?' She flashed her torch in the direction of the enclosure.

'No. And she didn't go for them last night either,' said Rick. 'Quite the opposite, in fact.'

'What do you mean?' asked Hank. 'She darned nearly pulled down the gate!'

'Yes, and she was trying again, just now,' Rick agreed. He looked Hank straight in the eye. 'Most mothers would.'

'Mother?' echoed the producer. 'You mean, that lioness is the mother of my cubs? No, no. She can't be. Their mother's dead.'

'I don't think so,' Rick said, and he explained what he'd concluded from the lioness's actions.

'You mean she tracked the cubs all the way here and now she's trying to take them?' asked Brandon, looking dumbfounded.

Rick nodded.

'I don't believe it! It's impossible,' scoffed Hank.

'It sounds incredible,' Sophie breathed. 'I wish I'd been there to see it. Do you think she'll come back?'

'Not so soon after she's been frightened off,' answered Rick. 'Tomorrow night, perhaps. And then you can see for yourself.'

'I'd like to see that, too,' said Hank.

'Well, you can join us in the hide tomorrow night,' Rick said to him. 'But bear in mind you'll be safer in your tent.'

'I'll take the risk,' said Hank thoughtfully.

Rick radioed the other askaris posted around the site and asked them to make sure the lioness was no longer in the camp. Then he and Benjamin went to check the area around the enclosure.

'I hope your dad's right,' Sophie said to Jake while they waited for Rick to return. 'It would be fantastic if Marigold and Marmaduke got to be with their mother again.'

'Oh, he's right,' Jake assured her.

Half an hour later, with everyone in the camp reassured that the guards were ready should the lioness return, Rick, Jake and Shani headed home in the Land Rover.

'What are you going to do about her?' Jake asked

Rick as they drove along the black and silent track. Having seen her at such close quarters, he knew just how dangerous she was. What if she wandered in to camp again while someone was going out to the bathroom tent?

Rick concentrated on the winding, bumpy road and said quietly, 'I'll have to trap her.'

'And then what?' asked Shani.

'Once she's in the crate, we'll put her in the enclosure with the cubs,' replied Rick. 'That way we can be a hundred per cent sure she means them no harm.'

'And if we're wrong?' Jake gulped, having sudden misgivings as he remembered the strength of the lioness.

'Then we'll have to remove the crate and transport her far away – maybe even to another reserve,' said Rick. 'But I don't think we're wrong. We'll observe her for a while, then release her into the enclosure with the cubs.'

'Great!' exclaimed Shani. 'I can't wait to see that.'

'You might have to wait, if things don't go smoothly,' Rick told her. 'There are no guarantees that we'll catch her. Also, it's going to be very dangerous. You saw how ferocious she was.'

Despite Rick's warning, Jake felt his heart pound

at the thought of trapping the lioness. There was a special game capture unit at Musabi that caught animals in the reserve for relocation to other parks. It was extremely risky work that required both skill and experience. Jake hadn't been out with the capture unit yet. Now, at last, his chance had come to see them in action. And they'd be catching one of the most awesome creatures on the African continent!

TEN

Jake gripped a corner of the big wooden crate, his hands already damp with heat inside the thick leather gloves. Three members of the game capture unit took hold of the other corners of the trap, which was on the back of the truck close to the cubs' enclosure.

It was late afternoon of the following day and the Musabi team had assembled at the camp. The damaged fence around the enclosure had been mended once more, and the only sign of last night's attack was a dark patch of dried blood on the ground – blood from the lioness's wound.

Jake glanced at the stain and shivered. Hopefully no more blood would flow that night.

'*Tayari*?' asked the ranger opposite Jake.

Jake nodded. 'Yes, ready.'

'OK. Lift!' ordered the man.

Jake and the three men dragged the heavy cage off the truck and put it on the ground next to the fence, upwind of the hide.

'Do you really think the lioness will go inside *that*?' Shani asked Jake. She wrinkled her nose as she studied the crate. 'I wouldn't!'

Jake had to agree with her. The gate, especially, was unwelcoming. It was made out of heavy steel bars, making it impossible for anything inside to escape.

'She'll go in if she's hungry enough,' Rick promised, coming over to join them. 'And seeing her leave the cubs to go after that warthog last night, I'm pretty sure she is hungry,' he added. He pushed up the gate until it clicked open, then he took out a huge piece of raw meat from a cooler box and flung it to the back of the crate.

Jake's mum, Hannah, took a photograph of the baited crate. She had brought her camera to make a record of the night's events. Like everyone else, she had been astonished at the possibility that an injured lioness had tracked down her cubs far from their original nursery site.

'Who's going to shut the gate when she goes in?' asked Shani.

'No one,' Rick told her. 'It drops down automatically when an animal enters.'

'So we could end up catching a hyena or a jackal, or anything else that smells the meat,' observed Shani.

'That's right,' Rick told her. 'Maybe even the wrong lion!'

'Crumbs! I didn't think of that,' Jake said. 'Then what?'

'We release it and hope it beats a hasty retreat,' said Rick. 'Then set the trap again. Of course, there's always the chance the lioness won't come back. She's been scared off two nights in a row, remember.'

'She *will* come,' said Shani, her brown eyes serious. 'She wants her babies back.'

Inside the enclosure, Sophie and Brandon were feeding the cubs. The little lions seemed happy to ignore all the activity outside while they were drinking. But as soon as they'd drained their bottles, they sat bolt upright and watched the proceedings, their heads tilted to one side with curiosity.

'We're doing all this so that you can see your mom again,' murmured Brandon, stroking Marigold's head. He glanced over at Jake and shrugged. 'Well, we *hope* it's their mom.'

The sun quickly dropped below the horizon and Rick asked one of his team to park the truck out of sight. 'And you two can call Mr Alderton to say everything's ready,' he told Jake and Shani.

They ran over to the producer's tent. Hank was waiting for them, dressed from head to foot in camouflage gear. Like Hannah, he was carrying a camera.

When Hank saw the impressive steel cage, his eyes opened wide. 'She's sure to be wild when she finds herself caught in there,' he remarked. 'I'll need to get some good shots so the folks back home can see what a great target she would have been!'

Rick shook his head slowly. 'This is serious and risky work, Hank,' he said tensely. 'Not just a photo opportunity.'

'Yeah, right,' said Hank but Jake could see the producer had already forgotten how frightening it was to have an angry lion in the camp.

Jake and Shani clambered up into the hide behind Rick and Hannah. It wasn't big enough to accommodate everyone, so the three men from the capture unit offered to watch from the branches of a massive fig tree that overhung the enclosure.

'Good idea,' said Brandon. 'Is it safe to join them?' he called up to Rick.

'Should be,' answered Rick. 'They're all armed. But you'll need to keep really still up there.'

'Will do,' said Brandon, and he jogged over to the tree and athletically scaled the trunk.

From the ground, Sophie watched him swing hand over hand along a branch. 'Tarzan!' she teased, flashing him a smile before climbing up into the hide to join Hank and the Bermans.

'I suppose that makes you Jane?' Hannah laughed lightly.

'Not quite,' grinned Sophie, hauling herself on to the platform.

Jake settled down in a corner, unwrapping a sandwich to quiet his rumbling stomach. He knew from experience that they could be in for a long wait.

One by one, the lamps in the camp went out as the calls of nocturnal animals signalled the start of the wildlife night shift in Musabi. A rustling movement in a clump of tall dry grass made everyone stiffen. But it wasn't the visitor they were waiting for.

'Just a bat-eared fox,' Jake whispered to Shani, as the little hunter emerged. Drawn to the strong smell of meat, the tiny fox looked round cautiously then sneaked towards the trap.

'Shoo!' said Rick, clapping his hands, and the little carnivore – whose ears seemed too big for its body – darted away in fright.

Gradually the moon rose, bathing the savannah in

a silver sheet of light. And into that light, as suddenly and silently as before, came the faithful lioness.

Jake felt a line of sweat break out on his forehead. He watched her limp warily up the slope, her head held low as she scanned her surroundings, alert for even the tiniest movement. At the top, she stopped and pricked up her ears then looked up at the hide. Jake dug his fingernails into his palms, terrified she'd seen them.

The lioness fixed her gaze on the platform and sniffed the air. In the hide, the atmosphere was thick with tension. Sweat dripped down from Jake's forehead into his eyes, yet he dared not even blink in case the lioness saw the minute movement. After several long seconds, she lost interest in the hide and went on again, moving unwaveringly towards the enclosure, and the trap.

The lioness stopped a few metres from the crate and stared at it. With the tantalizing scent of fresh meat filling her senses, she looked torn between the promise of food and the desperate cries of her cubs.

Go for the meat, Jake willed her silently.

Inching forward, the lioness approached the trap. She padded around it, sniffing suspiciously, then, finding the entrance, she gave way to her desperate hunger and hesitantly went inside.

Crash! The iron gate slid down, shutting her in. Inside, the lioness exploded, hissing and growling ferociously as she rammed at the bars with her front paws, making the crate rock violently.

Hearing her made the cubs cry out in distress. They charged back and forth next to the fence, their hackles raised and eyes wide with fear.

'Time to go,' said Rick, signalling to his team in the fig tree. 'The rest of you, wait in the hide.'

'Can't I come with you?' objected Hank, lifting his camera.

'Later!' Rick told him, climbing to the ground. He approached the crate cautiously, his gun raised and the three rangers at his side.

'I guess they have to be careful in case the gate isn't properly shut,' whispered Shani.

Jake nodded, his heart thudding painfully in his chest.

As the four men came closer, the lioness threw herself at the bars again, snarling savagely.

'Wow!' breathed Hank. 'She's no pushover! Nothing like the sagging old creature I was expecting.'

'She's superb!' agreed Hannah quietly. 'And amazingly strong, considering her injury.' She raised her camera and focussed on the scene below with a powerful zoom lens specially adapted for night-time photography.

Jake saw Sophie put a hand on Hank's arm. 'You could never destroy such a magnificent animal, Hank,' she murmured.

Hank looked at her but said nothing. Then he took the lens cap off his camera. 'I'd better take whatever shots I can, too.'

Rick was now standing beside the crate, his gun still raised. The lioness had sunk to her belly and was growling and hissing angrily at him. With one quick movement, Rick tested the gate. The lioness sprang to her feet and latched on to the bars with her massive jaws. The gate stayed shut.

Rick jumped backwards then signalled to Sophie and Brandon. 'She's furious but at least she can't get out. We need to move fast. See if you two can get the cubs to the back of the enclosure, so we can carry the crate in.'

'This isn't going to be easy,' Sophie muttered, looking over her shoulder at the bewildered cubs as she climbed down from the hide.

'Shani and I could help,' Jake offered. He called to Rick. 'Can we help with the cubs?'

Rick nodded. 'OK, if it speeds things up. But be careful. They won't want to be handled right now.'

Jake scrambled down the scaffold with Shani close behind him. Being careful not to let the cubs run out, they slipped through the gate into the enclosure with Sophie and Brandon.

As Sophie had predicted, it wasn't easy to get the cubs to the other side. With the lioness so close, Marigold and Marmaduke refused to leave the fence, striking out and snarling at anyone who tried to pick them up.

Jake made a grab for the loose skin at the back of Marmaduke's neck, but the fiery little lion spun round and clawed Jake's arm. 'Ouch!' Jake winced. He glanced across to Rick who was standing next to the crate looking very tense. Rick waved his hands, urging Jake and the others to hurry up.

'We're doing our best,' Jake muttered, bending to pick up Marmaduke again. This time, he managed to close his hands round the cub's middle, but only briefly, before Marmaduke twisted himself free once more.

Sophie pulled some dried meat out of her pocket. 'Let's see if this helps,' she said, holding it out towards the cubs.

But the excited pair didn't even look at the meat. They were interested only in the crate outside where the lioness was still thrashing around noisily in a desperate effort to escape. Jake groaned with frustration as he caught Rick's impatient eye again. He knew the cubs wanted to get to the lioness, but they were slowing everything up. 'Now, look, you two,' he said, 'you'll just have to co-operate if you want to be with your mum again.'

'No chance of that,' said Sophie. 'We'll have to outsmart them.'

'We could try wrapping something round them,' Jake suggested, 'so that they can't move their legs.' He pulled off his sweatshirt. 'Let's try this.'

'It's worth a shot,' said Sophie.

Jake dropped the sweatshirt on top of Marigold. It covered her almost completely, making her stop dead for a moment. Quickly, Jake picked her up, wrapping the shirt tightly round her so that her thrashing legs were pinned close to her body.

'Great job, Jake,' said Brandon, pulling off his own sweater and creeping up on Marmaduke.

Moments later, the little male was in Sophie's arms, securely wrapped up like his sister.

Shani looked at Jake and Brandon. 'You two will smell like lions when you get your shirts back.'

'And the cubs will smell like Jake and Brandon,' Sophie pointed out with a frown.

'Won't that put the mother off?' asked Shani, looking worried.

'Or make her attack them?' Jake added. He remembered reading something about animals rejecting their young if they'd been handled too much by humans.

'I don't know,' Sophie admitted, shaking her head. 'Let's hope not.'

With the cubs finally under control, it was time to move the trapped lioness into the enclosure. Holding Marigold firmly in his arms, Jake watched from the back of the enclosure as Rick and his men strained to lift the crate. But with a three hundred pound lioness thrashing about angrily inside, it was impossible to get it off the ground. Rick stood up, sweat pouring down his face. He wiped the back of his hand across his forehead and called out, 'Give us a hand will you, Hank and Brandon,' then added, 'and you too, Jake.'

Carefully, so that the sweatshirt wouldn't work loose, Jake handed Marigold to Shani and sprinted over to the crate. Brandon didn't hesitate either, but Hank looked taken aback. 'Are you sure it's safe?' he called to Rick.

'Right now, yes,' Rick replied through gritted teeth.

Growling and spitting with rage, the lioness craned her neck towards Jake as he approached. She bared her razor-sharp teeth – teeth designed to rip and tear the flesh of her victim. Jake's eyes met hers and for a split second she held his gaze before she raked at the steel bars with a huge paw, her claws almost grazing Jake's face.

'Ready, guys,' Rick prepared them. 'OK. Let's go!'

Bracing himself, Jake heaved at the crate, his muscles straining and his cheek pressed against the wooden panels. Inside, the lioness whirled around, pounding at the sides then attacking the bars again. The heavy box bucked under the shifting weight. Jake staggered and thought he might lose his grip, but he managed to regain his balance just as the others began moving towards the gate. Awkwardly, he shuffled sideways through the narrow gap and let out a sigh of relief when Rick called to them to lower the crate just inside the fence.

'Right, back to your places all of you,' Rick ordered once the box was on the ground.

Jake shook his stinging hands and made for the gate, looking back once at the lioness. She was panting heavily and staring at him with a look of confusion and anger. Jake suddenly felt a wave of pity for her. She'd suffered so much torment it was no wonder she was mad with fury. 'Don't worry,' he murmured to her. 'Everything's going to be all right.'

Then he hurried out and hoisted himself into the hide.

Down in the enclosure, Rick climbed on top of the lioness's crate and tied a long rope to the barred gate then hurled the other end over the fence. Next, he signalled to Shani and Sophie who were still holding the struggling cubs. 'Time to let them go.' He leaped off the crate and waited for them outside the gate.

'We'll leave them wrapped up so that we have enough time to get out before they reach the lioness,' Sophie called over to Rick.

'OK,' Rick responded. 'And we'll all need to be out of sight by that stage.'

While the cubs wriggled madly to free themselves, Shani and Sophie ran outside. Rick locked the gate securely behind them. 'Into the hide, you two. And make sure everyone keeps quiet,' he added, before picking up the end of the rope and hiding behind a bush.

Sophie and Shani had just reached the platform when the cubs finally shook off the shirts and went bounding over to the crate.

Jake could sense everyone holding their breath as they looked down at the moonlit scene. Even though Rick was convinced the lioness was the cubs' mother, no one could predict how she would react when the three were finally reunited. And what about the human scent from Jake and Brandon's shirts? Would this make the lioness even angrier?

The cubs reached the crate and pushed themselves against the bars, whimpering as they tried to find a way in. Jake could just see the lioness's massive head behind the steel gate. The moment she saw the cubs, she twisted round and lay down so that her belly faced the clamouring pair.

Jake could hardly believe his eyes. Far from rejecting the cubs because they carried the smell of humans, she was trying to let them suckle!

He glanced down at Rick hiding behind the bush, and caught his eye. Rick nodded once. It seemed this was all the evidence he needed. Slowly, he pulled on the rope, raising the iron grid that separated the lions. Jake felt Shani gripping his arm, her fingernails digging into his skin, while on his other side, Brandon put one arm round Sophie's waist and breathed in deeply.

The cubs needed no second invitation. The moment the gap was big enough, they crowded into the crate. A series of excited growls and yelps filtered out.

Jake had never felt so relieved in his life. He glanced at Rick again. His stepdad raised a thumb at him but his face was still lined with worry. Jake knew that the situation was far from over. The lioness might have accepted her cubs, but this meant she'd probably be more protective than before – and a lot more dangerous.

Everyone waited in silence. After a while, the lioness peered out warily from the crate then stood up and padded into the open. In her mouth, she carried the meat Rick had used as bait. The cubs tumbled out next to her, leaping up at her sides.

The big cat headed straight to the fence then worked her way round the perimeter, testing the wire again and again as she looked for a way out. Jake wondered if Rick would open the gate and let the small pride go, but his stepdad just continued to watch them.

Lashing her tail angrily, the lioness made a last-ditch attempt to escape. Near where Rick was hiding, she stood up on her hind legs, gripped the wire tightly with her front paws, and, with the meat still dangling from her mouth, tried to climb the fence.

'No!' Jake croaked, suddenly terrified now for Rick hiding behind the bush.

But the fence was too high, and the lioness was distracted anyway by her cubs who were still jumping up at her, trying to suckle. Growling softly, she dropped on to all fours. With a resigned look on her face, she stared out towards the river then slumped down on her side and began to tear at the meat.

The cubs flopped down next to her, and Marmaduke stretched across to sniff at the lump of raw flesh in his mother's claws. She licked his ear then gently butted him away with her head. Marmaduke looked surprised, but the message was clear. The meat was hers! Turning away, he clambered over her front legs and began to suckle, snuggling up against Marigold who was already feeding contentedly.

Jake swallowed hard. 'It's probably her first meal in days,' he murmured, as the lioness tore into the meat.

'And it's the cubs' first *real* feed in days, too,' whispered Shani in a choked-up voice.

Hank was transfixed. 'This is pure Hollywood,' he breathed. 'I couldn't have written a better ending myself.' He turned to Sophie. 'You said something to me earlier about not destroying her.'

Jake closed his eyes and waited for Hank to continue. Surely he wasn't going to start talking about shooting this magnificent creature now? Shani, clearly on tenterhooks too, dug her nails deeper into Jake's forearm.

'Well, I won't,' the producer announced, and Jake had to suppress a cheer that welled up in him as Hank continued enthusiastically, 'that was just incredible! I never thought animals could show such emotion. You could practically read that lioness's mind.' He lifted his camera and focussed it on the little family. As the shutter clicked, Hank said the words Jake had hoped to hear. 'The hunt's off. From now on, I'll stick to shooting with my camera.'

ELEVEN

'*Hakuna matata?*' Jake called over to the askari in the camp car park. It was early the next day, and Jake and Shani had arrived with Rick to feed the lioness.

The guard gave him a wide grin. 'No problem. The lions slept well all night. So did Bwana Alderton – after his *karamu.*'

'He had a feast?' asked Shani, puzzled.

'Not a proper one,' replied the askari. 'But after you all left, he sat for a long time drinking a glass of wine. He looked very happy – like a man does when he's celebrating something.'

'He should have been celebrating,' said Shani. 'For the lions.'

'And also because he was so lucky to see that brilliant reunion,' Jake added as he helped Rick take the cooler box out of the Land Rover. Now there was the next phase of the operation to look forward to. Last night, on the way home, Rick had said he wanted the lions to stay in the enclosure for a day or two. This would give the mother a chance to regain some of her strength. But as soon as she was stronger, Rick would release them into the bush.

They left the askari and walked across to the tented area.

'Morning, all,' Hank called out, emerging from his tent with Felicia and Raquel. 'Great action last night, wasn't it?'

'Yes, indeed,' said Rick, letting go of the handle of the cooler box as he and Jake put it on the ground. 'We were really lucky to see it.'

Sophie and Brandon came out of the kitchen tent, each with a glass of orange juice.

'Hi there,' said Sophie. She looked at the cooler box. 'More lion food, I take it?'

'Uh-huh,' Jake said.

'The lioness has certainly earned a good meal or two,' remarked Brandon. He smiled at Sophie. 'Isn't it going to be cool to see them heading back into the wild?'

'Maybe,' said Hank before Sophie could respond. His eyes glittered with excitement. 'But actually, I've decided they'll be coming home with us.'

Jake stared at Hank. 'Going home with you?' he echoed, before he could stop himself. He shot a troubled glance at Rick, who looked just as appalled.

'You can't be serious, Hank!' said Rick.

'Oh, I am,' smiled the producer. 'There's plenty of room for them on our ranch in California. Just imagine – a whole family of lions straight from Africa!' He beamed at Felicia. 'I planned it all last night. And to think Bill Carter only has a leopard!'

Felicia rolled her eyes. 'Why do we have to be one up on our neighbours all the time?' she asked Hank. 'Can't you think of a better souvenir? Something that's harmless.'

'Yes. These are dangerous animals, Hank,' Rick reminded him firmly.

The producer dismissed Rick's concern with a nonchalant shrug of his shoulders. 'Maybe,' he said. 'But this little pride is so unique, I've just got to have them. Like Rick said just now, it's not every day you see such an amazing reunion between wild animals.'

Jake caught Shani's eye and raised his eyebrows in exasperation.

Raquel had been listening patiently to the conversation. Now, her eyes lit up and she began tugging at her father's arm. 'We're going to have three lions!' she said excitedly.

'That's right, sweetie,' said Hank. 'And we could even carry on filming them at home if we need more shots for the movie.' He beckoned expansively to them all. 'Come on, everyone, let's go and have a look at our magnificent trio.' With one arm round Felicia's waist and the other resting on Raquel's shoulders, he set off for the enclosure.

Jake gave Rick a desperate look as they picked up the cooler box. Mr Alderton had to be stopped. 'You should have let them go last night,' he muttered to Rick. 'Now look what's happened.'

'Don't tell me what I should have done,' Rick replied quietly, narrowing his eyes.

Jake knew he'd overstepped the mark. After all, his stepdad was the expert here, and this gave Jake a flicker of hope. Maybe Rick would still be able to persuade Hank that the lions should go free.

Jake and his dad strode past the others and rounded the shade cloth first. As everyone else caught up, Rick signalled to them to stop. 'This is close enough,' he warned. 'We don't want to stress the lioness by going too near.'

The lioness's keen senses had alerted her to the

group's arrival even before she'd seen them. She was standing near the fence, staring out at them. Her unblinking amber eyes gave nothing away, but Jake could see that every muscle in her body was taut so that she could spring into action if she had to.

'She's not stressed,' objected Hank. 'She looks totally cool.' He took a step forward, but Rick grabbed his arm.

'Don't!' he said and as if to underline this, the lioness suddenly bared her teeth in warning and snarled menacingly.

Hank stepped back again. 'She's pretty mean,' he breathed.

'Yeah. Not an animal to be trifled with,' said Brandon, a look of awe on his face.

'I guess after her gentleness with the cubs last night, I kind of forgot about the wild side of her,' said Hank. He turned to Felicia. 'But I'm sure she'll get used to us eventually.'

'You really think so?' challenged Felicia, looking doubtful.

'Absolutely,' said Hank. He glanced at Raquel, who seemed to have grown bored and was dangling from the lowest branch of a nearby tree. 'Careful, honey,' he said. 'And let's not forget,' he went on, 'that I legally own these three lions. Those rangers from Kasaba – Havers and Lawson – will confirm that I've paid the reserve handsomely for all three. So I might as well keep them.'

A big knot of frustration formed in Jake's stomach. The producer had an answer to everything!

'If we're talking legal,' Rick warned, 'then I think you should check out Havers and Lawson more closely. You'll probably find they don't have the authority to arrange hunts in Kasaba.'

'Sure they have,' retorted Hank, just as Raquel launched herself off the branch and landed with a thud on the ground right next to the fence.

In a flash, the lioness was on her feet. Roaring savagely, she charged over to Raquel, slamming into the fence and kicking up a huge cloud of dust as she skidded to a halt. The dust enveloped Raquel who was rooted to the spot almost within reach of the lioness's claws, screaming in terror.

For a second, everyone was frozen in horror until Hank came to his senses and raced over to Raquel. He scooped her up in his arms then backed quickly away saying, 'It's OK, sweetheart, it's OK. She can't get out, I promise.' But his trembling voice suggested that he wasn't at all sure the lioness couldn't force her way through.

Jake was filled with the same doubts. It had been bad enough when the lioness had tried to break in to the cubs the other night. But this time, the force of her charge had seemed so much stronger. She wasn't going to let anything come near her cubs.

The lioness eyed Hank and Raquel for a few more seconds, then turned and padded quietly back to her cubs.

Sweating profusely, Hank carried Raquel over to Felicia who was looking shocked and very angry. She pulled Raquel away from Hank and held her protectively. 'You'd better be right about that, Hank,' she said, her face flushed. 'What if the lion *had* managed to get out?'

The producer turned to Rick, his face pale. 'Maybe the mother would be too much of a handful,' he croaked.

Jake held his breath. The penny had dropped at last! Mr Alderton had seen just how wild the lions were. But as the producer continued, Jake's heart sank again. 'So perhaps we'll just stick with the first plan,' Hank went on. 'To take the cubs home, but not the lioness.'

'You can't!' Jake cut in impulsively, feeling like he could thump something – or someone. 'Not now that they're back with their mother.'

Brandon then stepped forward. 'I'll second that,' he said. 'These are wild creatures, Hank. If you insist on taking them away from their home, I'll cancel my contract for this movie!'

'And I'll sue you for breach of contract,' Hank shot back, the colour returning to his face.

'Do it then,' Brandon said calmly. 'You still won't have me in the movie.'

Way to go, Brandon, Jake wanted to shout out. He guessed that if Brandon pulled out of the movie, it might not turn out to be the blockbuster Mr Alderton was hoping for.

Mr Alderton and Brandon faced each other squarely for a few moments, neither of them saying anything. Eventually, though, it was Hank who broke the stalemate. Shaking his head, he reached across and put his hand on Raquel's curly head. 'I guess I could live without the cubs,' he said. 'But I promised Raquel she could have them and I can't disappoint her.'

Shani jabbed Jake with her elbow. Jake understood. If Hank knew what had happened to Raquel in the enclosure the other day, he might change his mind about keeping the cubs. He wondered if he should say something, but Raquel beat him to it. Calmly, now that she was safe again, she looked at her father. 'But I don't want them any more, Daddy,' she said, scrunching up her face. 'They need to stay in Africa with their mom.'

Jake let out a long breath and glanced sideways at Shani. Her brown eyes danced back at him.

Hank raised his eyebrows. 'Do you mean that, sweetheart? You really don't want the cubs to live on our ranch?'

Raquel nodded vigorously. 'Can I have a kitten instead?' she asked.

'Of course. You can have as many as you like,' Hank said but, catching Felicia's disapproving eye, he added, 'Well, maybe just one for the time being. And now I think you and Mommy need to get ready for your next scene. Filming starts in an hour.'

Turning quickly, Raquel tripped over a big stone and nearly fell into a thorn bush. Jake stepped forward and grabbed her arm just in time.

'Careful, Raquel,' Felicia said anxiously. 'You don't want any more scratches on your arms and legs.'

Shani shot an amused glance at Jake who was struggling to keep a straight face. He quickly looked away and said to Rick, 'Can we feed the lioness now?'

'Sure,' said Rick. 'Help yourself.'

Jake took a huge lump of meat out of the cooler box. Grimacing, he tossed it over the fence to the lioness. It landed with a thud in front of her. Grabbing it with one huge paw, she began to devour it, keeping her wary amber gaze on the small crowd observing her. The cubs grew excited when they smelled the meat and tried to nose their way in for a share.

'There's some more in the box for them,' Rick said, nodding to Jake.

Jake and Shani took out two smaller lumps of meat and flung them over the fence. The cubs sprang away from their mother and fell hungrily upon the unexpected bonanza.

'I guess that's how they'll be fed at Rungwa,' observed Hank. 'They won't need to hunt for themselves once they're at the animal sanctuary.'

'Rungwa?' Sophie echoed, looking surprised. 'Who said they're going to Rungwa?'

'Well, no one, yet,' replied Hank. 'But we still need them for the movie. By the time we're finished, they'll be pretty used to humans so I guess they'll have to go to a sanctuary – as we planned originally.' He looked at Rick. 'You can't really release semi-tame animals back into the wild, can you?'

'You can't tame them any more!' Jake burst out. 'It would be all wrong.'

Rick wiped his hands on a broad leaf that he plucked from the fig tree. 'Jake's right, you know, Hank. It wouldn't be fair to keep treating these cubs like film stars. The lioness could end up rejecting them altogether.'

Rick's argument failed to move Hank. 'Look, sorry guys. I can't help that,' he said. 'I've agreed to let the lions stay in Africa, but I've got a movie to make and I can't pull out of it now. Like everyone else,' he added, giving Brandon a fleeting look, 'the cubs have to finish their contract!' He caught sight of Shani's horrified expression and shrugged. 'I know you only want what's best for them, but Rungwa's not a bad option when you think about it. The three of them will be pretty safe. No killer buffaloes, for starters.'

'No freedom either,' murmured Jake to Rick.

Hank overheard him. 'Maybe it's better to be safe than free,' he said with a shrug. 'And now, I must check what's happening on set. See you all later,' he called as he strode away.

Jake and Shani stared after him. 'He just won't give in,' muttered Shani.

'Well, that's what makes him such a successful movie producer,' Sophie pointed out.

In the enclosure, Marigold and Marmaduke were squabbling over a small piece of meat. Marmaduke was lying down, jealously guarding the dirt-encrusted lump of impala flesh in his front paws. Marigold biffed him across the head with her unsheathed claws then lunged. Her brother lifted his lip and growled at her, then grabbed the meat in his jaws and ran off, with Marigold bounding after him.

'Marmaduke's just like Hank,' Brandon laughed. 'He won't give in either!'

Except that Marmaduke has to be stubborn like that so he can survive in the wild, Jake thought.

Sophie was watching the cubs' behaviour closely. 'It's fascinating how they have all the right instincts,' she observed, echoing Jake's thoughts.

'But they're not going to get the chance to use them,' Jake pointed out.

'I don't know about that,' Sophie said thoughtfully, as Marigold leaped on to her brother's back and bowled him over.

'You mean you can make Hank change his mind?' asked Rick, picking up the cooler box to take it back to the Land Rover.

'I hope so,' answered Sophie.

Jake felt a ray of hope. 'What are you going to do?' he asked.

'I don't want to say just yet,' Sophie told him. 'But keep your fingers crossed, everyone.' She took Brandon's hand and started for the film set. 'Come on, Brandon. You and I have some extra work to do.'

TWELVE

Later that day, back at the Bermans' house, Jake and Shani were feeding Bina on the veranda when they heard the sound of an approaching vehicle.

'Who's that?' Jake wondered, jumping on to the wall to get a better view of the road. A cloud of dust mushroomed into the air above the dirt track, coming closer as the vehicle sped along. Shading his eyes with his hand, Jake could see a small green jeep at the head of the dust cloud.

The jeep disappeared for a few moments as it turned into the Bermans' drive then came into view once more when it rumbled over the cattle grid and into the front garden.

'It's Sophie and Brandon,' Jake said, jumping down from the wall. 'I hope they've come to tell us Mr Alderton's going to let the lions go.'

He ran to meet them. Shani followed, carrying

Bina who was still latched on to the teat of her bottle.

'Oh, isn't she the cutest little thing!' Sophie exclaimed when she saw the tiny dik-dik. 'May I hold her?'

'Sure,' said Shani, handing the antelope to Sophie.

Even though she was still feeding, Bina didn't seem at all disturbed to find herself in a stranger's arms. 'How long have you had her?' asked Sophie, stroking Bina's smooth brown forehead.

'About a week,' Jake answered. He explained how the dik-dik had come to be living with them. 'Rick says she'll never be able to fend for herself in the wild,' he finished. 'Just like Marigold and Marmaduke if Mr Alderton insists on taming them any more.' He looked hopefully at Sophie. 'So what's the news?'

'Well, nothing concrete yet,' Sophie answered, and Jake felt a moment's disappointment. 'But Brandon and I are pretty optimistic our plan will work. We'll tell you all about it in a minute. First we need to clear something with your dad. Is he here?'

'Yes, he's in the office,' Jake said.

Rick's office was a small thatched rondavel some distance from the main house. It stood at the top of a slope near the back fence, overlooking a wide river plain that was a favourite gathering place for elephants. Large herds spent hours cooling themselves in the muddy water, or browsing on the succulent trees growing on the banks.

Today, the elephants were there. Sophie and Brandon gasped in admiration as they reached the crest of the slope and saw the grey mass moving silently about.

'Wow!' said Brandon. 'I've never seen so many elephants before.'

Jake felt a rush of pride. He could still hardly believe this was his home now! He opened the office door.

Rick was talking on the phone. He held up one hand to show he wouldn't be long. 'Thanks, Lakakin. I'll wait to hear from you,' he said, then hung up. 'Hello. What brings you two here?' he asked Sophie and Brandon.

'Nothing concrete yet, but we need to ask you a favour,' said Sophie, still holding Bina. 'Do you think you could rig up another hide at the enclosure this afternoon? The first one's a bit high for our purposes. We need one at ground level, close to the fence, with gaps in the sides for camera lenses.'

Jake was intrigued. Clearly Sophie wanted to film the cubs in their enclosure. But how would this tie in with the film? He perched on Rick's desk, waiting to hear the plan.

'Another hide's no problem,' said Rick. He pointed to the chairs in front of his desk. 'Take a seat and tell me what you have in mind.'

Sophie sat down and looked at Brandon. 'You explain,' she smiled at him, 'seeing as you were responsible for the finer details.'

'Well, basically,' said the actor, turning the other chair round and sitting astride it, 'we're going to change the plot.'

'You mean, have a whole new movie?' asked Shani, leaning against a tall filing cabinet.

'That's about it,' Brandon nodded. 'And it's going to be even better than the original. In fact, it's going to be based on a true story.'

'Whose story?' Jake asked, leaning forward with his elbows on his knees.

'All of ours,' said Brandon. 'You, us, the lions. We're going to shift the emphasis of the movie. Instead of dealing with a pair of cubs living with the hero and his girlfriend, we're going to show the same couple rehabilitating the orphans back into the wild.'

Shani frowned. 'But if they're going to be released, why do you need to film them in the enclosure?' she asked.

'So that we can show every stage of the release,' explained Sophie.

'I get it!' Jake said. 'You want to take lots of shots of the cubs practising their hunting and stalking skills.'

'Exactly,' said Sophie. 'Like we saw them doing today.' She put Bina down on the floor. The dik-dik sniffed around then made a beeline for the door.

'No, you don't,' said Shani, running after Bina and picking her up. *'You're* not going back into the bush.'

'What does Hank think of your idea?' asked Rick, leaning back in his chair.

'We haven't told him yet,' Sophie admitted. 'We wanted to have everything OK'd by you first.'

Brandon reached across and took Sophie's hand. 'Won't it be great?' he said enthusiastically. 'We'll be dealing with issues that really matter.'

'You sound just like Hannah.' Rick grinned and looked at his watch. 'Now, if this hide's to be ready in a few hours, I'd better get on to it right away.'

'And we'll go and see if Hank will listen to our plan,' declared Sophie.

Soon after lunch, Jake, Rick and Shani arrived back at the camp with all the equipment needed for the second hide. They left it in the Land Rover and went to find Sophie and Brandon.

They were sitting at the table under the trees with Hank and Felicia. From a distance, Jake tried to read the producer's expression. Did he know of the plan yet? But Hank's face gave nothing away.

'Back to feed the lioness already?' called Hank, waving.

'Er, no,' said Rick, shooting Sophie and Brandon a glance as he walked over to the table. 'We're here to erect a hide next to the lions' enclosure.'

Hank looked puzzled but before he could say anything, Sophie interjected. 'It's part of what we wanted to discuss with you, Hank,' she said, and she started to outline the script change they had in mind.

The producer listened in silence. When Sophie finished, he leaned across the table to pour himself some wine. Jake watched him tensely. Mr Alderton *had* to see what a brilliant movie it could be.

The producer took a mouthful of wine then offered the bottle to Rick, who declined with a shake of his head.

'Oh, for heaven's sake, Hank,' Felicia said suddenly, breaking the tense atmosphere and voicing Jake's feelings of frustration. 'Stop playing games with us. You know Sophie and Brandon have come up with a winner. Just say so!'

Hank put down his glass then sat back and folded his arms. 'It's a good story,' he finally agreed. 'But . . .' he paused and Jake readied himself for a big let-down. 'But I don't know if the backers will agree to it. They've put their money on something totally different.'

'They've put their money on you as the producer, and me and Brandon as the stars,' retorted Felicia. 'They know only too well that we can turn just about anything into a blockbuster. And another thing,' she added, pointing to a magazine she'd been reading, 'we need to move with the times.' Jake glanced at the title of the magazine. *Your World Now*, he read.

'What do you mean, Felicia?' asked Hank, pulling out a chair for Raquel as she came running over to join them.

'People everywhere are becoming very aware of the environment,' said Felicia. 'And I think we should too.'

Hank thought for a moment. Finally, he said to Rick, 'Will this second hide allow us to get close-up, ground-level shots of the cubs?'

'Oh, sure,' Rick told him.

Hank took a deep breath and shook his head. Raquel stretched across the table, trying to reach the magazine. 'Here, honey,' said Hank, passing it to her.

Then he turned to Sophie. 'It looks like I'm outnumbered,' he said with a wry grin.

Jake felt as if he'd just passed a really tough exam. 'Thanks, Mr Alderton,' he said, a huge smile stretching across his face.

'You're a star!' burst out Shani, and she threw her arms around the producer and hugged him tightly.

The seasoned Hollywood businessman seemed touched. He returned the hug then, releasing Shani, he said, 'Thanks, sweetheart. But you should thank Felicia too.' He glanced at his wife.

Felicia gave him one of her most dazzling smiles. 'Someone has to win! So it might as well be me,' she said. She put her hand on Raquel's arm. 'Are you taking notes, honey?' she teased.

Raquel nodded solemnly without looking up from a spectacular photograph of a herd of wildebeest.

As far as Jake was concerned, however, the real winners here were the lions. 'When are you going to start filming the cubs again?' he asked Hank. He figured that the sooner filming began, the sooner the lions could be released.

'Just as soon as the hide's up,' replied Hank.

'So what are we waiting for?' Jake said to Rick.

Hank drained his glass and pushed back his chair. 'While you're setting up, the rest of us can start working on the script changes. At least this time the cubs can improvise as much as they like!'

Jake went with Rick and Shani and one of the askaris to put up the hide. It was made of brown tent canvas and it ran the length and breadth of the enclosure just centimetres from the fence so that the cameras could focus through the wire. At regular intervals, there were gaps in the canvas. Some of these were about a metre from the ground and others only about half a metre to allow for shots from different angles and heights.

The lions watched the activity outside their enclosure with wary interest. As usual, the mother was on edge, her whole body tense as she kept watch over her cubs. Several times, when people came too close to the enclosure, she erupted with anger, and charged the fence to drive them off.

With each attack, Jake grew more concerned. He kept thinking about Rick's remark that the lioness could reject her cubs if she got too distressed. But Rick was cautiously optimistic. 'It's not for long,' he said when the hide was finally ready and he was standing inside with Jake and Shani, looking through one of the viewing gaps into the enclosure.

Jake peered through another gap at the little family that was lying together in a golden heap looking like any pride of lions whiling away the hot afternoon hours. Only the fence told otherwise.

They went back to the tents where Hank was briefing the cameramen. 'All ready?' he asked as Rick approached.

Rick nodded. 'We'll leave you to it,' he said. 'As soon as you're finished filming, we'll get ready for the lions' release.'

'It'll take some planning on our side, too,' Hank pointed out. 'It'll be the only chance we'll get to film that. Unless,' he grinned at Jake and Shani, 'you two are prepared to keep bringing the cubs back until we get a perfect take!'

'Oh sure. That'll be dead easy,' Jake laughed.

A truck pulling up in the car park drew everyone's attention. 'Who's that?' Brandon wondered, putting down his cup.

'Oh, no!' Hank groaned as two familiar figures climbed out of the vehicle and headed over. They wore tan-coloured camouflage gear and carried rifles. 'Lawson and Havers. They must be here for the hunt. In all the excitement, I forgot to tell them it was off.' He pushed back his chair and went to meet the men. 'Er, look,' he began. 'There's been a change of plan. I'm sorry. I should have told you earlier.'

The two men were clearly put out by Hank's announcement. 'You can't back out of our agreement now, Mr Alderton,' argued Lyle Havers.

Hank folded his arms. 'But, guys, there's no lioness to hunt now.'

'Oh, that's no problem,' said Russell Lawson quickly. 'We'll identify another one soon enough.'

'Actually, that's not the point,' said Hank. 'After everything I've seen here, I'm not interested in killing animals any more.'

Jake and Shani exchanged a look of victory.

'So you can refund the fee that Hank paid you, gentlemen,' interjected Felicia calmly.

Havers and Lawson looked taken aback. 'Er. That might be a bit hard to arrange,' Lyle stuttered. 'We, er, I mean, our boss at Kasaba will have banked it already.'

Rick stepped forward. 'He hasn't. I spoke to Lakakin on the phone this morning. He knows nothing about the money, the hunt or any orphaned cubs.'

Russell and Lyle's faces dropped. 'He's probably forgotten,' Russell muttered. 'He's a very busy man.'

'Not too busy to check up on what's going on,' Jake said, seeing a jeep pull up next to the pick-up truck. His keen eyes had already spotted the

Kasaba motif on the front doors, and he recognized the tall, lean man even before he climbed out of the jeep. It was Lakakin Mukuli, the head ranger at Kasaba.

Suddenly looking nervous, Lawson and Havers hurried over to meet their boss. Mr Mukuli stopped, a stern expression on his face. The three were mostly out of everyone's earshot but Jake picked up one or two words. Phrases like *no authority, not another chance* and *dismissed.* Then the two rangers climbed into their truck and drove away without a backward glance. Jake suspected that was the last anyone would see of them.

Rick introduced Lakakin Mukuli to everyone. 'I'm sorry my men deceived you,' the dark-skinned, regal-looking man said to Hank. 'They were acting without my knowledge.'

'The rotten liars!' said Shani with feeling. 'I hope they're going to pay for all their fibs.'

'Let's put it this way,' Lakakin told her. 'They won't be arranging hunts at Kasaba again.'

'And the money I paid them?' asked Hank.

'Don't worry, Mr Alderton. The cheque will be here in the morning,' Lakakin reassured him.

'Oh, but Hank doesn't really want it back,' Felicia put in. 'Do you, honey?'

Hank looked at his wife in surprise. She beamed at him and Hank shrugged. 'Apparently not.'

'He wants to donate it to Kasaba,' continued Felicia. 'Don't you, sweetheart?'

'Apparently I do,' said the producer, shaking his head with amusement.

The filming of the cubs went ahead without a hitch. Over the next two days, Jake and Shani watched as Marigold and Marmaduke unconsciously acted out their new parts with flawless instincts. The camera crew captured the pair wrestling, stalking, leaping, prowling – actions that the cubs would practise to perfection as they grew into adults.

The lioness was still intent on getting out, and tested the fence regularly to see if she could push her way through. Because of this, Rick posted a team of guards to keep a round-the-clock watch on the enclosure, and he was in constant radio contact with them in case anything went wrong. He and his men also had to keep checking the wire to make sure it was still holding, and every time they did the lioness would run wildly at them, roaring and snarling with terrifying intent.

'You'd think she'd settle down a little bit,' Jake remarked once to Shani after one such incident, 'especially with all the free meat she keeps finding in the enclosure.'

'She'll never settle, Jake,' Shani reminded him softly. 'Not until she's in charge of her own life again.'

'Yeah, I know,' Jake agreed.

Behind the fence, the lioness was staring at Jake with cool, amber eyes – the eyes of a predator at the top of the food chain. Jake tried to look away but found himself locked into her unwavering gaze. He couldn't even blink. 'Just as well the filming's nearly finished,' he murmured to Shani as they walked away.

When the crew wasn't busy filming, they were quietly packing up the camp. Jake and Shani lent a hand. On one occasion, they were helping to dismantle the veranda set when Jake found a single guineafowl feather lying on a chair. He felt a pang of regret. It had been brilliant helping out on a real movie set and meeting world-famous film stars. Maybe he should keep the feather as a souvenir.

Just then, the feather drifted to the ground, landing next to a dung beetle that was pushing a ball of dung with its back legs. The comical sight of the beetle walking backwards on its front legs while pushing a ball several times its own size made Jake chuckle.

Life was certainly never dull at Musabi. Even the insects were fascinating! But as the beetle rolled the ball of dung straight over the feather, Jake decided he wouldn't keep it as a souvenir after all.

On the last day of filming, the ground-level hide was dismantled, and all the tents were taken down and packed away on a fleet of hired trucks. The lorries then headed off for the airport at Dar es Salaam, taking most of the crew and actors.

'You'd never know a whole movie company had been here, would you?' Jake said to Shani as they walked around the clearing where the façade of the house had been. Apart from a lot of footprints in the dust and some patches of flattened grass, the site had gone back to the wild. Jake picked up a plastic coffee cup that someone had overlooked and stuffed it into his rucksack. It looked so out of place now against the brown sand and dusty bushes.

A light breeze rippled through the branches of the fever trees. Two warthogs appeared from behind a bush but, seeing the humans, they quickly turned and scurried away. 'It's all right. You'll be able to come back later,' Shani called after them.

A loud *whoosh* accompanied by a raucous chorus of *waak-waak-waak* sounded in the air above Jake and Shani. *'Hono hondo kijuvu,'* said Shani, pointing to a flock of about fifteen silvery-cheeked hornbills landing in the trees.

'It sounds like they're pleased they can roost up there in peace tonight,' Jake said as he and Shani made their way over to the lions' enclosure for the last time. He looked towards the western horizon. The sky was streaked with pink and orange as the sun sank lower. It would soon be dark. Impatiently Jake craned his neck towards the road. 'I wish Rick would hurry up,' he said. 'Otherwise it'll be too dark to film the lions leaving.'

With the camp dismantled except for the original hide, the shade cloth screen and the enclosure, and only the Aldertons, Sophie and Brandon left, the final scene was scheduled for that same evening. Hank had decided to film it himself, to save needing another cameraman. The camera was already up in the hide, mounted on a tripod.

Rick and Hannah eventually arrived in good time. Rick drove the Land Rover over to the enclosure and parked near the gate. 'There's only room for a few in the hide,' he said joining the others behind the shade cloth. 'The rest will have to watch from my vehicle.'

'That's fine by me. I'll take shots from the window,' said Hannah. 'I'll be able to get some superb close-ups.'

Felicia and Raquel were also happy to sit inside the sturdy vehicle. 'I think it'll be much safer here than up on the platform,' said Felicia, climbing inside and locking the door.

'Probably,' agreed Rick. 'But I don't think the lioness will even bother to look at the hide. She'll want to get out of here pretty fast.'

Jake was glad to hear this, especially as he preferred to be able to watch from the hide. He was sure they'd see a lot more from there. 'Is there room for me and Shani?' he asked Rick hopefully.

'Yes,' replied Rick. 'I'll be manning the gate, then making a run for the Land Rover.'

'Rather you than me,' commented Hank.

Quietly they all went to their respective places. Jake hauled himself up the scaffold. *For the last time, I hope*, he told himself. At the top he looked down at the three lions. The mother was crouching at the back of the enclosure, her body tense as if she was preparing for the hunt. Jake wondered if she sensed what was about to happen. Next to her, the cubs lay sprawled out, completely unaware of how much their lives were about to change.

Hank focussed his camera then signalled to Rick that he was ready. The breeze had dropped and nothing else stirred. Even the birds were silent. It was as if the whole reserve was holding its breath, waiting for the release.

Rick walked over to the gate. The big cat pricked up her ears and tracked Rick's movements with her hard, cold stare while rising silently to her feet – a lioness preparing to stalk her victim.

Rick reached the gate. He quietly unlocked the padlock then slid back the bolt and swung open the gate. It clanged noisily against the post, making the fence shudder. The lioness snarled menacingly and darted forward a few paces. Jake's heart skipped a beat, but Rick was already safe, having sprinted to the safety of the Land Rover.

Now the camp belonged to the lioness and her cubs. She fixed her steely gaze on the open gate as if to make sure Rick was no longer there, then she lifted her head and sniffed the air. Behind her, Marigold and Marmaduke lay watching, their little heads cocked to one side.

Limping over to the gate, the lioness peered out cautiously. She waited and listened, then stared hard at the Land Rover. Inside, no one moved.

Go on, Jake willed her silently. *You can go home now.*

The lioness looked back over her wounded shoulder at her cubs and growled softly.

'You tell 'em,' whispered Hank, looking through the camera. 'Tell 'em it's time to go back into the wild, where they belong.'

In that moment, Jake knew that the American had finally understood the true nature of the lions.

Down in the enclosure, the cubs jumped up and scampered to their mother. She bent her neck and licked them both on their heads, then, holding her tail in the air like a flag, she loped through the gate. Outside, she paused and looked straight up at the hide.

Jake heard Sophie take a deep breath and he was sure he could hear her heart beating. Then he realized it was his own heart pounding like a drum.

The lioness stared suspiciously at the platform. She wrinkled her broad scarred nose as she tested the air again then suddenly let out a deafening roar.

Again and again, the lioness roared into the gathering night, then, her signal sent, she whirled round and headed for the river, her cubs trotting confidently behind her. Across the glinting thread of water lay Kasaba. The lioness was taking her cubs home.

'*Uhuru*,' whispered Shani next to Jake.

'Yes. Freedom,' Jake echoed softly, just as the

tawny cubs and their mother merged with the darkening, gold-tinted bush and disappeared from sight.

This series is dedicated to Virginia McKenna and Bill Travers, founders of the Born Free Foundation, and to George and Joy Adamson, who inspired them and so many others to love and respect wild animals. If you would like to find out more about the work of the Born Free Foundation, please visit their website, www.bornfree.org.uk, or call 01403 240170.

HUNTED
Safari Summer 2

Lucy Daniels

Living on a game reserve brings Jake Berman face to face with animals in the wild. It's exciting – and dangerous – but Jake's always ready for adventure . . .

Jake is thrilled to be going to a chimp conservation area. But gunshots on his first night in the jungle make him realize that it's more dangerous than he thought – and for the chimps most of all. He and his friend Ross are determined to stop the hunters, no matter what the risk . . .

TUSK
Safari Summer 3

Lucy Daniels

Living on a game reserve brings Jake Berman face to face with animals in the wild. It's exciting – and dangerous – but Jake's always ready for adventure . . .

Jake can't believe his luck – an elephant relocation programme has chosen his parents' reserve for rehoming a family of elephants. Tracking elephants by helicopter is right up Jake's street! But soon Jake finds himself risking everything to protect the relocated family from their greatest enemy – ivory poachers.